JAN -- 2017

Also by Ainslie Hogarth

The Lonely

eats?

THE BOY
MEETS GIRL
MASSACRE

(Anotated)

n

Ainslie Hogarth

eats?

THE BOY
MEETS GIRL

MASSACRE

(Anotated)
n

flux®
Woodbury, Minnesota

First Edition
First Printing, 2015

Book design by Bob Gaul
Cover design by Ellen Lawson
Cover image: iStockphoto.com/22094427/©sorendls
　　　　　　iStockphoto.com/34933692/©Miroslav Boskov

Flux, an imprint of Llewellyn Worldwide Ltd.

Library of Congress Cataloging-in-Publication Data
Hogarth, Ainslie.
　The Boy Meets Girl massacre (annotated)/Ainslie Hogarth.—First edition.
　　　pages cm
　Summary: "When sixteen-year old Noelle takes a summer nightshift job at the Boy Meets Girl Inn, the site of a decades-old murder, she keeps a diary to document evidence of hauntings, until another ghoulish murder lands her diary in the hands of investigators"—Provided by publisher.
　ISBN 978-0-7387-4472-8
　[1. Haunted places—Fiction. 2. Diaries—Fiction. 3. Murder—Fiction.
4. Summer employment—Fiction.] I. Title.
　PZ7.H68319Bo 2015
　[Fic]—dc23
　　　　　　　　　　　　　　　　　　　　　　　　2015014187

Flux
Llewellyn Worldwide Ltd.
2143 Wooddale Drive
Woodbury, MN 55125-2989
www.fluxnow.com

Printed in the United States of America

For Deb and Tom,
the best parents a weirdo could ask for.
I love you guys.

DP | **DALRYMPLE PRODUCTIONS**
1200 Sanderson Blvd, West Hollywood, CA 90069, 981-555-0189

Dear Detective Umbridge,

I first met Trevor Donald at a coffee shop a few months ago. He was one of those men who looked just thoroughly exhausted. Like a rag used too long to wipe tables at a diner, loose and greasy and frayed at the edges so the only solution is to throw it out and get a new one. We got our coffees to go and sat outside while he smoked cigarettes and told me a little about himself.

I often find myself in situations like this, occupying sticky tables in dim bars or too-bright coffee shops with eager storytellers, mostly full of shit. I do this to feel superior to other creative execs, even though these meetings rarely result in an actual movie. But Trevor was different. He didn't try to sell it to me. Instead he was just very upfront about needing the money and wanting me to read it for myself. Of course this non-pitch intrigued me more than any pitch I'd ever heard in my life.

Sorry, what he had wasn't actually a script. Rather, a diary. What we call "source material." This diary was a piece of evidence he'd found at a grisly crime scene back in the '90s. A piece of evidence that he'd become more or less obsessed with. His words. He admitted the diary was part of the reason he lost his job as a detective. Part of the reason he didn't leave the house much these days and his ex-wife hadn't spoken to him in over a decade.

Since I was looking at this project to cut my teeth as a director, I asked if getting so involved with the diary would ruin me too, and he laughed and shrugged and said he couldn't make any guarantees, then handed me a large yellow envelope.

What the envelope contained wasn't the *actual* diary, of course. He didn't have it. What he gave me was a copy. A printout, transcribed and annotated by Trevor himself for expert analysis back in 1999; child psychologists, handwriting specialists, even a paranormal investigator looked at it. He told me the original diary was probably still sitting in a plastic bag, isolated, tucked away in some cold evidence room in King City. That's exactly how he put it. Like it was a shame or something, that it was sitting all alone in that small room.

Anyway, I read the diary and loved it. My boss read the diary and loved it. In fact, he loved it so much he immediately approved a generous finder's fee for Trevor and agreed to give him an associate producer credit if he wanted it. He was that sure this thing would be a success. I wrote Trevor a few production notes on the printout, mailed it back to him, and called him right away to tell him we wanted it, pending the notes he'd find in the manuscript, of course—things we wanted to change, you know, things we had to nail down to guarantee it'd be a moneymaker. I didn't know who else he'd shown it to, if there was some other company in the loop that had a vision more in sync with Trevor's, though I don't think he really had a vision at all. I asked him to look at my notes and let me know what he thought. Call me or write me if he had any ideas of his own, that kind of thing. Anyway, he was thrilled, I was thrilled.

He called me a few days later and left a message that said, "I found the kid." And that was all. You'll see what that means in the diary.

Then I guess after that he disappeared.

I was sad, you know? I'd only met him once, of course, and we'd spoken just a few times on the phone, but he seemed like a good man. And a good detective, based on his old annotations in the diary. I liked the guy. I really did. Is a detective always a detective, even after they retire? Like a doctor is always a doctor, or a judge is always a judge? If not, I think they should be.

Anyway, I'm ashamed to admit that we were moving on to development without him when you contacted our office. We've selected a screenwriter, acquired financing, my boss has approved me to direct. We even have a few Noelles in mind.

I'm happy to cooperate and put a hold on production for the time being. I am. Trevor brought us this idea, so it's the least we can do. However, I want to make it very clear that we're not legally bound to do this and therefore can only justify it for a short period of time. We'll stop, effective immediately, out of respect for Trevor and your department, but you've got to understand, and I hope you don't find this insensitive, we couldn't even *invent* better publicity at this stage—the lead detective on the case has gone missing, for god's sake—so we'll be moving forward into pre-production in a month's time.

That's pretty much all the information I have on Trevor, but feel free to contact me again if you've got any more questions. Like I said, we're happy to cooperate. And as per your request, I've mailed you a recording of that last message Trevor left on my machine, a photocopy of the annotated source material he originally gave me, including my notes (sorry, it was the cleanest copy we had), and also a cover letter Trevor had enclosed in that yellow envelope way back when. This letter will be the first thing you see when you open the package.

I hope you find what you're looking for in there.

The very best of luck,
Roger Dalrymple

Hello Mr. Dalrymple,

The author of the following diary never willed it to anyone, nor did she have any close relatives interested in collecting her personal items, so it effectively became "public" as soon as it was admitted to evidence at the trial. Of course the actual "public" has to jump through about a dozen hoops to see these kinds of "public" documents, complete a mountain of forms, gather endless signatures, that kind of thing. But that's a different conversation altogether.

As the lead detective, I worked very closely with this document. This diary. In fact, since I first pulled it blood-soaked from an evidence bag and began reading, not a day goes by that I don't think about the girl who wrote it. Noelle Dixon. Maybe a murderer. Maybe not. Even after all these years I still don't know.

As you see, the diary you've got here isn't the original, or even a photocopy of the original. I typed up this copy back in 1999, and added a bunch of footnotes—information I'd picked up from locals, handwriting experts, etc. The footnotes were intended to aid the child psychologists who lent their expertise to our department. I've left them in for you, in case you get confused or have questions. Or you can just ignore them if you want.

I don't want to come off as desperate or unhinged—I assure you I'm no more desperate or unhinged than the next retired cop—but I *need* you to take this project. I *need* this diary to be out of my hands. I need it gone. Dead. Killed by a movie. So please, no offence, but feel free to butcher it any way you want to. And I'll do anything I can to help.

I'd moved with my wife to King City just three months before the murders occurred. Promoted to detective if I could relocate, so I did. Then on September 1st, 1999, at 8:48 a.m., an employee from The Boy Meets Girl Inn phoned the King City Police Department and reported a scene so ghoulish that Linda, our dispatcher, initially took it for a prank. Some kid putting on a voice and calling on a dare. I'd been warned about the day after the Anniversary. Linda told me there'd be calls like that all day. You'll see why when you read.

So anyway, as per procedure, she sent an officer over anyway, warning him that there was a good chance he'd be mooned. She told us she'd chuckled at her own joke as his car pulled out of the lot.

When the officer arrived, Jessica West, our caller, sat on the front steps. Eyes wide, fingers twisted together tight as rope. She'd phoned inn manager Olivia Grieves too, who sat next to her, rubbing her back, her head dropped into a sun-shielding hand, the first two fingers occupied with a cigarette steadily burning, the smoke catching the light, dancing to some slow, strange tune. That was exactly how the officer put it to me, about her cigarette smoke. He didn't last too long on the force.

Anyway, he said he knew right away that it wasn't a prank; both women looked too pale for such a warm, sunny day, sitting before the inn's gaping double-doors. It was a mansion really. Over a hundred and fifty years old, with big, flat, rectangular expanses of red brick and what seemed like hundreds of white-shuttered windows. For your movie, though, it probably doesn't matter how it really looked.

But it's important to know it was warm out. A sunny day. The wrong kind of day to find what he found just inside those double doors.

In the lobby, twin girls lay side-by-side on a blood-soaked carpet, face up, arms tucked in, torsos resembling salsa: piles of coarsely chopped flesh and fat and blood and bone.

The officer said he'd initially thought they'd been killed with, he shuddered as he recounted, "a chain saw."

A bloody trail led up the stairs, but, he recalled noticing, "no footprints."

Two more bodies were found in a bed. A boy and a girl. Fewer perforations than the bodies

7

downstairs. Less concentrated. The officer could see distinct though irregularly shaped holes in the bodies; wide, unclean gouges. "An axe," he now theorized.

But not quite.

More blood, leading to another room where one of the nightshift kids, Alfred Gustafson, had been impaled with the same instrument, so many times in the throat that he'd been nearly decapitated, his jaw torn from his head in the process, blended into the mess separating his body from his still face.

The officer, coming back down to call the station, noticed a door beneath the stairs, a closet, from which swelled a pool of blood that reached all the way to other side of the hall.

Bracing himself, he opened it and found the other nightshift kid, Noelle Dixon. Sitting on a stool. A pickaxe lodged into her skull and propping her body up like a picture frame.

A pickaxe.

What had made those wide, unclean gouges, those irregularly shaped holes in the five other bodies: this pickaxe.

At her feet lay a diary, splayed open on its front, the covers protecting its pages from the blood that glazed half of Noelle's head and dripped heavy from her chin. The diary almost appeared to be in its own little

pool of blood, as though it too had been
killed in the night.

That diary's contents are what follow.

Yours sincerely,
Detective Trevor Donald

First Entry[1]

You're new to me, diary. I've never had anything like you before.

Alf and I both went out and bought something like you before starting our night-shift jobs at the inn, to document all the weird stuff that might happen. Like, you know, doors slamming, cupboards creaking open all slow and creepy, the piano playing itself, all the usual haunted house stuff.

We didn't buy them together either, since we didn't even know each other yet. Not really, anyway. Just each other's names from going to the same school. The diary thing

---

1 Numbered entries indicate where Noelle seems to have started a new section. Because none of the entries are dated it's difficult to determine how much time elapsed between each, or whether or not entries were made on the same day.

came up on our first day. Except Alf called his a JOURNAL, because boys don't have DIARIES, and sometimes Alf could be lame like that. But not often.

Anyway, it feels weird to just pick up and start doing something like this when you've never ever done it before.

That's why I avoided using you for the first month or so of working here.

You're green and very smooth and embossed in gold on your spine is the word "DIARY," I guess just in case someone tried to use you for any other reason. And you're not hard, either. You're bendy and you're small so I can fit you in my hoodie pocket all the time.

You're very beautiful actually.

Anyway, I had to pick you up today because last night, for the first time, something seriously, actually crazy happened.

I mean, there's been a few sort of weird things already. One spot in the hallway is freezing cold for no reason, Alf thought he lost his favorite hat and then it reappeared, sitting on top of his bag one morning. There was this weird smell coming out of one of the kitchen cupboards, Alf swore up and down it smelled like rotting flesh even though he has no idea what that would smell like. The smell went away after a few hours and hasn't been back since.

But last night was different. I was lying in bed, kind of drifting off to sleep, when suddenly my room got very cold. Too cold. It kind of takes a while to realize that a room is just way, way too cold, a lot of feet kicking and hoisting up the blankets and curling up in a ball, thinking that's all it's gonna take to be warm. But then I could see my breath, full clouds at first, then scared, shallow puffs, because I knew something was about to happen. And suddenly my bathroom light turned on. And it stayed on. And it was aggressive. Almost daring me to go turn it off.

From my bed the open bathroom door shows the whole sink and part of the toilet. Hidden behind the open door is the shower. After a few seconds of what felt like a staring contest with the lit-up bathroom, the door slowly began to move, creaking loud to a close, all the way, so I heard the latch catch. As though something standing in the shower had pushed it all the way shut.

I yanked my blanket up over my nose and stared at the closed door without blinking until my eyes just about dried up and I had to shut them. I kept them shut, more wide awake than I'd ever been beneath, and I thought I could hear whispering. But it was so faint, too faint, I couldn't be sure. Probably I was just terrified. Probably I was hearing things.

Somehow I eventually fell asleep because there was nothing else to do under those blankets and those closed eyelids.

The next morning I told Alf about the bathroom door and he was jealous and he said, "Write it down, write it down!"

I said, "You write stuff down too. You write about your hat."

But he said that he feels "like a girl" writing in his diary. I said, "I thought yours was a JOURNAL," and then we laughed because usually Alf is pretty good at laughing at himself and I'm pretty good at making fun of him.

It kind of sucks that something like that happened right in my room, though, because actually I spend a lot of time in there. More time than Olivia, our boss, realizes. I shouldn't have written that down. Now if she ever finds this diary she'll know how much I slack off. But actually Olivia would never read this. She's an honorable old bat. I just called her an old bat. There's another reason I really hope she doesn't open this thing up.

See, I have to spend a lot of time in my room because I've got this sore spot in my brain.[2] And sometimes it hurts so bad I can barely stand it. Not like a headache really. More like the way a canker sore hurts and can hijack your whole mouth. Every other part of my brain won't stop tonguing and probing and prodding it. And it can kind of feel good, the way tonguing a canker sore can sometimes feel good, white hot pain almost savory. But also terrible like a canker sore. And distracting like a canker sore.

And when my brain's canker sore flares up like that it helps to lie on a bed on my stomach with my face turned to the side, my cheek all squished up into my eye so it doesn't really work right and everything gets fuzzy. I leave a light on somewhere, something weak so everything in the room is just warm, and I look sort of down into the bedspread so that the pattern on it begins to melt and stretch open. My squished cheek goes numb, my lips pushed up and plugging my nostrils so I've gotta breathe loud cold air through my teeth.

It's not like regular daydreaming.

I'm not thinking of any one particular

We'll use voiceover narration for some of this early stuff.

---

2 A postmortem CT scan revealed no irregularities.

thing, like, you know, I'm not thinking of a particular kind of life I'll have when I grow up, when I leave the house, when I'm so pretty that nothing else matters.

It's more that I'm just thinking about *feeling* good. Good feelings. That blissful blip between starting to piss the bed, letting it out and loving it, and realizing you're pissing the bed, cold and wet and having to get up now and deal with it.

Slowly I begin to seep through the cracks in the bedspread's pattern, then emerge whole on the other side, inside the pattern, floating through patterned space as though on an inner tube.

Patterned space is the perfect temperature, moist-warm insides of a just-done cake; patterned space enters my body and fills it up and spills back out again, scary at first but just for a split second, and then you let it happen, filling up and spilling out and filling and spilling over and over and it's just so wonderful you never wanna breathe real air again. You wanna die. Because maybe if you die in patterned space you get to stay there forever and it'd be worth the risk.

And the best part of all is, amidst all the filling and spilling of patterned space, my sore brain just kind of vaporizes. And it hisses out of my ears like really a satisfying fart. The kind of fart that may as well be a dump, it feels so good. Then there's nothing at all left in my head. Once filled with sore brain, now cool and empty.

It's the best feeling in the world.

But then it always happens that like, in the distance I'll hear something, like a drop of water fall into a puddle, and it echoes. And I know the good feelings are over. I'm suddenly extracted from patterned space; I'm a dark swirl sucked into a needle then spat back out on the bed. Because that sound, a drop of water in a puddle sound, it MEANS EMPTY. Instead of BEING EMPTY.

Because BEING EMPTY means there's no puddle of water to hear at all.

The bedspreads at home are old and soft and pilled and peach-colored with big turquoise paisley. Bald spots in the stuffing and weird fishing wire poking out everywhere. Because we're poor and we don't have money to buy better blankets, but whatever.

This is great. ——— That's not me. I'm not a poor person.
People love
poor kids.

I like the bedspreads at the hotel but they're not great either. They're actually not as soft as the bedspreads at home, even though they're definitely more expensive.

Stuffing quilted tightly put; dense patterns of busy greens and pinks and yellows.

Anyway, like I said, I take a lot of breaks and I go and lie on them and try to do the same thing with them, like, let my ears fart.

Sorry, diary, that was pretty weird.

Actually wait, did I just apologize to a diary? Why would I make my diary so easy to offend? We're gonna have to thicken that skin of yours. Otherwise you won't be able to handle this job. [3]

Alf, who you'll be hearing a lot about, I'm sure, his name is short for Alfred. Alfred Gustafson. Because I guess his parents hated him as soon as they saw him and wanted to ruin his life with the worst name in the world. It's the kind of name that's so powerfully terrible it could make a good-looking person seem ugly. Not that Alf really has to worry about that. He's just as ugly as his name.

---

3 Likely referring to her own job at the inn requiring a certain level of fortitude. The Boy Meets Girl Inn's grim history is well known throughout town. Over 150 years old and plagued with unusual tragedies, or in some cases the rumor of them; murder, suicide, torture, hundreds of sightings of "ghosts" and other strange phenomena. Most people in the area don't even like passing by it on the street, let alone spending long stretches inside or sleeping in it. I'll admit to feeling a certain level of unease when I first stepped inside the inn, however that could be due to the fact that the interior was still covered in bloodstains.

He's not actually. I'm kidding. Don't tell his JOURNAL, diary, if you guys, you know, swap stories, but actually Alf is a perfectly good-looking person beneath his bad haircut and his weird mannerisms and nerdy clothes.

Love interests — do not wear turtlenecks and sweat- pants. Even if they do.

Real nerdy, like sweatpants and turtlenecks and asthma. Not the way that some people wear, like, expensive vintage horror movie T-shirts or whatever and say like, "Oh I'm such a nerd for liking this super cool thing to like."

I make a lot of mean jokes like that, like, about his parents hating him and about him being ugly. I make fun of his walk too. He sort of has this way of walking on his toes that makes him look like an idiot. Between the tippy-toe walk and his name being Alfred, it's almost a crime not to make him fetch things for you like a butler.

And yeah okay I know I shouldn't be mean to him, and I swear, in the beginning I wasn't this bad. If I'm being honest for a minute he's probably actually my best friend, which seems crazy because we've only really known each other for a month, but I don't know, it's just what happened. And it's why, right now, I really can't help myself being extra mean to him, because right now he really does deserve it.

See, over the past couple weeks Alf has developed this idiotic crush on me. He hasn't said anything about it, but I can tell and it's not fair.

It's not fair because we were getting along fine as just friends. Better than fine. It's been great. But as usual, as soon as a boy can even have the slightest bit of conversation with a girl he would also have sex with he just ruins everything with a crush. Like friendships with girls aren't worth preserving somehow, they can be picked off and flicked away like flecks of skin, never safe, always worth ruining with a goddamn irresponsible crush.

And doesn't that make him kind of deserve it? Deserve my meanness? For only really looking at me like I'm some kind of sex hole? So much so that he'd risk our whole friendship just to be able to have sex with the sex hole. So much so that he hasn't even noticed what a terrible bitch I've been to him since his crush started showing. Or what a ridiculous couple we'd make. Like I could be anything at all around this hole and it really wouldn't matter. I could have six-inch serrated claws. I could have a mouth full of rotting, maggoty teeth.

I think it makes Alf worse than me. Even

though maybe to other people, I'm the one who looks like the asshole.

And I'm sure I'm just sensitive because I don't make friends that easily. In fact I don't make friends like Alf at all. Or maybe I like Alf too but don't wanna admit it because I don't wanna lose the realest friend I've ever had. And, this sounds terrible, but like, I'm a lot better-looking than he is. There. I said it. And I don't wanna hear it from you, diary, you know you'd feel the same way.

And like, obviously I'm not gonna marry a person that I date now, when I'm god-damn sixteen years old, so why ruin it? Why not just be friends forever? Doesn't he know how special we are? To be friends the way that we are?

And it makes me mad that I think that way because it means that I like Alf prob-ably way more than he likes me. If I'm wor-ried like this, about not being able to be friends forever, and he's not. He just gets to have his crush and be happy. He should just never have had the crush in the first place. Even now, just from writing that out, I'm angry with him. And I'm definitely going to be mean to him the next time I see him, whether I want to or not, goddammit.

ANYWAY.

The hotel we work at is called The Boy Meets Girl Inn. [4] The sign is this fluorescent honeymoon red, one of those signs that buzz all the time. And the M buzzes loudest because it's on the fritz, and every few seconds it burns out for an instant and so for a thousand and one instances throughout the day this place is called The Boy eets Girl Inn. The Boy Eats Girl Inn.

The Boy Meets Girl Inn. Potential title?

Which is actually a more fitting name when you think about it. [5]

But I don't really wanna think about it right now. I'll explain later, diary. I promise. I'll explain everything about the hotel so that you're good and ready for the rest of our summer on the nightshift. ————————

So, I know she might have killed everyone, but for the movie Noelle's our protagonist, not our slasher.

---

4 This name was part of an ill-conceived effort to rebrand the property as it transitioned from an apartment building into a "romantic getaway location" in 1986.

5 Reference to Margaret Grimley.

Second Entry

I'm not a virgin. There you go. Let's just get this out of the way now.

Noelle's gotta ——— I'm sixteen and I'm not a virgin.

be hot but
with some-
thing weird
about her; a
severe dye job
or big bags
under her eyes
maybe.

I lost it young but I can't really remember any details because I made myself EMPTY and stared into a bedspread.

I do remember that his name was Tucker and he was in grade eight and I talked him into it because I just wanted to do it and have it done with.

I wanted to get it done with because I guess I thought in some weird way it might feel good on my sore spot. A balm for it, sort of. Like, with Tucker, or anyone like him really (like, any boy), I could make myself more EMPTY than ever before. WHOLLY

22

TOTALLY ENTIRELY EMPTY for as long as it lasted.

So I guess I had weird expectations for my first time the way that other girls do, but not at all the WAY that other girls do.

I hate expectations. Any kind of expectation. They make it so you can't ever really experience anything in any real way; everything gets so muddled up. They're just not helpful, you know? They either make not great things seem better than they are, which isn't always good, or they create disappointment. Which is the worst feeling in the world.

I hope Tucker didn't have any big expectations.

I think even if he did have big expectations, he still would have done it with me because it would have been more important to him to tell all his friends about it, to be the first one out of anyone to have sex, than to actually have a good experience that met whatever EXPECTATIONS he might have had.

I know usually it's the other way around, some pervy older boy talking some younger girl into it, but not this time. This time I did the traumatizing. And I can tell I traumatized him too. Because these days that guy's stutter could move a sailboat and I don't think he's ever had a girlfriend.

— We're going to have to scrap all this touchy feely teenage stuff. That's what books are for.

23

SORRY TUCKER.

There. I feel better now actually. That's weird. Diary, you're like a priest and this is my confessional. How do I have to punish myself to make it right?

Waiting. Waiting.

Oh I see, your silence tells me that my life is punishment enough? Alright then. Fuck you, diary. You good for nothing bitch.

Oh god, here we go. Falling into the trap of the diary. What a goddam terrible idea, writing all of your most embarrassing and deepest and most terrible thoughts and feelings down in a book. Just begging to fall into the wrong hands. Why does anyone do this?

I mean, I guess it's kinda dangerous. That's sort of fun.

You're like a stick of dynamite, diary, just waiting to GO OFF in the wrong hands. Anyone could find you and you could potentially blow them away. Like if Alf could see all that stuff I wrote about him being a nerd and his parents hating him and stuff.

Anyway, my EXPECTATIONS of my FIRST TIME were met in that, it did feel good on that sore spot. I did go EMPTY like never before.

And in fact something even better than I could have EXPECTED happened.

After it was done and I kinda like, came back from the best EMPTY ever, I could feel the sore spot in my brain, right on my scalp. Migrated through my skull and all the way to the surface. I know that sounds fucking crazy, but it's true. This weird spot on my scalp that was kind of warmer and squishier, like a bruise on an apple, just appeared. Almost as though the tip of the sore spot in my brain were now peeking out, the way only a small part of an iceberg sticks out of the water. An access point. That I could press and feel kinda good. Not patterned space good, but pretty good.

So I started pressing on it all the time. When I felt weird or anxious or even just bored I pressed. Just pressing, pressing, making sure it was still there, still soft, as close to touching the soreness on my brain as possible. [6]

Anyway, it's not like I have sex all the time now or anything.

---

6 According to Jessica West and Olivia Grieves, this pressing on her head was a sort of twitch of Noelle's; something she did all the time almost unconsciously. We're still waiting on reports from the psychiatrists to confirm, but it seems to me to be, potentially, a kind of stereotypy or stim: "a repetitive movement, behavior, posture, action, or utterance; a kind of ritualistic self-stimulation that calms, or in some cases excites."

Third Entry

Alf and I learned a lot about each other pretty quickly. On the very first night we learned that the reason we'd both applied for the nightshift job was because neither of us likes being home much. Alf's parents actually do hate him. Which means I should probably NOT make fun of him for it. Like how you'd never make fun of an actual fat person for being fat.

I also learned that when he was five years old he watched his sister drown in the pool in their backyard. He sat on the highest accessible branch in their oak tree, paralyzed with laughter. A therapist would later tell him over and over again that paralyzing laughter is actually a very common reaction to extreme fear. But Alf told me that he wasn't afraid;

that he knew deep down that he was laughing because it was hilarious, because she was such an idiot, jumping in the deep end when she knew she couldn't swim, thrashing around like a fool, gasping for breath, spitting water, coughing. Of course he didn't realize then that she could die from drowning, that her body was doing anything and everything it could to preserve itself, not caring how hilarious it might look to basically imitate an inflatable advertising tube man catching the greatest wind of his life.

He says if he'd known that, that drowning would kill her, he would have done something to stop it. And because he knows that for sure, he's mostly okay about it. Which makes sense to me.

And his parents, they can't help hating him. And he gets that too, and appreciates how nice they are about it.

"I watched her walk up to the deep end," he said, "and I knew what she was going to do. And I wanted her to do it too. Because I knew it would be funny. I just, I hope she didn't see me laughing. I just hope that's not the last thing she remembers."

It was three o'clock in the morning on one of our first nights here when he told me that story. He said he'd never told anyone about the laughing before. He said usually when he told people that story, he was trying to get sympathy, or like, one-up someone who was trying to tell him that they had a fucked-up life. So he'd never mentioned the laughing, just that he watched her drown.

The good thing about Alfred is that it didn't seem to have ruined him in any obvious way.

Except for that he just wants to work at the inn for the rest of his life. I guess that's not normal.

The therapist also told his parents that often, Alfred's particular variety of trauma manifests itself as perfectionism, overachieving, being the best possible kid to make up for the fact that the other kid is dead. But Alf was the exact opposite. Too fundamentally lazy to have been broken that other, more common way.

The reason we were talking at three o'clock in the morning is because we'd both woken up from the noises. That was then, though, early in the summer. We're used to them now. The bumps in the night.[7]

---

7 Olivia Grieves suggested that these "bumps in the night" might be caused by a rat infestation, though empty traps in the attic and basement fail to prove such a theory and Olivia herself seemed skeptical of that explanation.

I didn't want to be at home because of my dad. Herman.

Herman has relentless bowel problems,[8] an unglamorous blood disease,[9] and heaps of credit card debt[10] that pester him almost as much as his physical ailments. We're totally poor because of him. Our house is small and kind of dirty and shitty. I told you about our thin bedspreads already. We eat a lot of fast food and ramen noodles and saltine crackers with peanut butter, and that kind of stuff keeps Herman's bowels irritable but it's all we can afford. I've had a job in one way or another since I was nine and Herman has been collecting disability and using it to keep giant packages containing utterly useless shit arriving on our doorstep since before I could remember.

At one point in his miserable life he'd actually been in line to inherit a car dealership from his father. He'd worked there since he graduated from college. But when my mother left he bungled it and then he got sick and started seeing specialists and naturopaths and

---

8 A spastic colon.

9 The blood tests are inconclusive at this point.

10 Herman Dixon was on a fixed government income due to his disabilities and also appeared to suffer from an addiction to buying infomercial products.

chiropractors and anyone at all who would promise to fix his blood and his bowels.

He told me before that he'd wished over and over again for a daughter. For me. For a little girl he could pour all of his love into without having to worry. Someone he could love as much as his wonderful wife. Ex-wife. That's why I'm here, because he wished for me. He didn't want to give any credit to my mother because she'd left us.

He always said, "I'm your mother and your father."

He was constantly calling the hotel, asking when I'd be home, telling me about his symptoms: "Noelle, it's liquid right now, absolute liquid. Like water. And it burns. My god how it burns. I don't know if it's connected to the blood but I'll tell you what, I'm wondering if it's made my sphincter as weak as the rest of my body. It affects the muscles, you know. And that's a muscle, just like any other muscle. And it takes the right muscles to keep it from just being liquid. You need the muscles to get the nutrients out and, you know, work it into a solid. Oh, Noelle. Oh god, Noelle. It's just so hard with you working nights. I wish you didn't have to. I miss you so much. I need you. I need you, Noelle. I ordered something that might help. It's this four-way massager that stimulates muscle development. Should be arriving tomorrow morning. When you get home we can target some of my weaker muscles, maybe you can help with the places I can't reach..."

And then the sore spot in my brain would flare up. I imagined it, pink to red and swollen and spewing something slimy. And I pressed and pressed and pressed harder, again and again, tided myself over until I could find some nice pattern to seep into.

God, it's so embarrassing.

So horribly, terribly, disgustingly embarrassing.

Diary, you dickhead, stop making me write these embarrassing things in you. How are you doing this? It feels good though, to write it down like this. Because when I write it down it seems like it can't be real. Like I'm a character in a movie, one of those princesses — *Ha!* whose mother died when she was young and left her with a terrible ogre of a father. Dead mother, ogre father, that's enough to make a person kind of special right? Though usually it's a stepfather, because the princess couldn't be the spawn of someone as absolutely terrible and disgusting as Herman. —————————

Depending how we play up the dad (sympathetic vs. monster), we could even get some critical attention.

Anyway, it still feels good in a way. I like it when you validate me, diary, when you confirm that my father is a terrible weirdo beast and that I'm special. I'm a princess. Keep that up and we'll be friends forever.

Man. I shouldn't have said that though. Any of that. About my dad. My poor, poor dad. He's got these watery eyes, all red-rimmed like the lids are turning inside out. I'm always sorry to see them open. That means he's awake. He's alive. Another day to endure. They're all yellow where they should be white and really they're sort of sickening but they make me depressed instead of nauseous.

It's not his fault he has the worst body in the world.

And I hate myself for hating him for it.

The other night he said, "Noelle, if I wasn't this way I could find someone to love. A wife to take care of me. Because, you know, this is a wife's job. A wife's job. This isn't your job. And I'm sorry for that, Noelle, you know I'm sorry, right? I'm not out of love yet, am I? I could find someone else. I could. I know it. And I know I'm a burden on you, sweetie. I have no right to do this to you. But who would want me this way? Who would want to take this on? I have no one else."

"Dad, it's okay. You're gonna be okay eventually, alright? And you're gonna find someone new."

"There's no one like your mother, kiddo."

"I know."

"She was too good for us."

"I know."

"So we can't hate her for leaving."

"I don't hate her, Dad."

"Aw Noelle. We're all each other has kiddo."

"I know, Dad."

That was a common sort of conversation. He repeated himself a lot. Because all he did was sit in the living room, scribbled in the TV's artificial light, getting fatter and fatter and fatter and fatter so if you fast-forwarded his life it would almost look as though he were melting into his armchair.

Sometimes instead of getting fatter in front of the TV, he'd get fatter on the phone. Sit in a creaking wooden chair in the kitchen, chatting with one of Dr. Schiller's [11] other chronically ill patients, because

---

11 The Dixons' family doctor. He'd been seeing Herman for the past 30 years and Noelle since she was a baby. He said Herman and Noelle had always been a "troubling pair," disclosing that Noelle came for physicals very sporadically, her father far too often, and that the last time he'd seen her was just a few days before the Anniversary. When asked if anything unusual happened during their appointment, he said that Noelle had seemed quite on edge, touching her scalp more often than usual. He also said that he'd spoken with her more candidly than ever before about her father's condition. He admitted that this only seemed to "agitate her more," and he regretted bringing it up.

that's all they had to talk about, all they had to identify themselves. HERMAN DIXON, Co., Bl. (that's colon and blood). He and the other patients would make a game of out-repulsing each other with gooey, stinky symptoms of their illnesses. Every minute growing less and less attractive to some potential new wife who might come and save me from hell.

Since I was little it's been all desperate clinging hugs, loud weeping into my shoulder, and stuff like:

"It's just you and me, Noelle."

"You're the only thing that keeps me going, Noelle."

"You're all I need in this world, Noelle."

In fact I can't think of a single day in which he hasn't said something like that. Or like:

"I'm sorry, Noelle."

"You don't deserve this, Noelle."

"I'm ruining your life, Noelle."

"You're my wish come true, Noelle."

He'd say that god wouldn't have given me a father like him if I couldn't handle it; that we were blessings for each other because he was making it so one day I'd be the best wife and mother in the world, teaching me to care for another person the way that I have for him. We were each other's precious gifts. He said, "Daughters end up marrying men just like their fathers, sweetie, and you're gonna make a man like me very happy one day."

It's weird to love someone for so long, really believe them that they're your whole world, and then suddenly hate them. A lot. And I know this is going to make me sound like an even bigger asshole, but like, it's hard to hate someone for something they can't help. It makes you feel really awful.

Like, it's really fucking hard to hate someone for their spastic colon. It really is.

It took a lot for me to finally admit it. Because it meant I basically had to admit that I'm a bad daughter. And a bad person.

I really wish he could have abused me in some more traditional way. Like if he beat me up or had sex with me or something. Because then I'd have a name to put on it, and years and years worth of Lifetime movies telling me that IT'S NOT MY FAULT and that HE'S WRONG. But this way of being treated, this was uncharted mental torture, it felt like a crime but it wasn't a crime because if it was a crime some nice-smelling social worker could legally take me away and I wouldn't have to feel so goddamn guilty.

I won't work at the inn forever and ever like Alf because I want to make enough money to run away and leave him. I'm okay that everyone in this town will think I'm an asshole because after I leave I'll never come back. I'll be LEGENDARY as an asshole. NOELLE DIXON LEFT HER POOR SICK FATHER AT HOME, SAD, LONELY MAN, HIS ONLY DAUGHTER THE BIG-GEST ASSHOLE OF ALL TIME.

And I'm never going to get married. I'm never going to have kids. I want everything about my life to end with me because I should have never been born. Never should have been wished for.

I'd initially thought that taking the night-shift at the inn would make it better, if we were on totally different schedules things might not be so bad. Maybe I'd miss him and start remembering things that I'd once loved about him. Slowly the absence would chisel away my hatred and I could see him as just a sad, sick man again.

But it was really only getting worse. His usual neediness laced with resentment that I was never around. I was getting less sleep and feeling more stressed so every time he said my name I wanted to feel his teeth

crack beneath my sturdiest boot. The nightshift — *The Night-*
just made me hate him more.

shift. Another

potential

title?

Do you wanna know what he did last
night? Okay listen to this. He called the
inn to tell me that he'd fallen and hurt his
back and couldn't get up and if I didn't come
home right away to help him he'd be stuck
on the floor, cold and alone all night long,
nowhere near a TV. He literally shrieked into
the phone.

So I rushed home, leaving Alf all alone
at the inn, which is honestly the worst even
though he was really nice about it, just to
help stupid Herman into bed, prepare a
hot water bottle or something, prop him in
front of a TV. Anyway, as soon as I opened
the door, I caught him walking out of the
bathroom. The sound of the flushing toilet
seemed to go on forever, fuelling my fury.

"Um, hi," I said. "What the fuck?"

"Oh, I ah, wow, Noelle, you left right
away for me?"

"You said it was an emergency, Herman."

"Honey, that's so sweet.

"Herman, I left work, Alf's there all
alone, I—"

"I just, I feel better now. I just kind of
turned and my back cracked and now it feels

better. So, I'm sorry, I would have called but I had to use the bathroom."

"You're lying."

"I'm not, Noelle, now don't you call me a liar."

"You needy, pathetic liar."

"Noelle!"

"You called me home from work, Herman."

"I swear I fell, my back was aching! It was!"

"Stop lying!"

"Here," and he rushed over to his bag and pulled out his wallet and produced fourteen dollars. "Here, why don't you run across the street and grab us a pizza, Noelle. The People's Court is starting in five minutes. We can have a nice night in now that you're home, okay? I'm sorry."

"I'm going back to work."

"No! Noelle, just stay home! You're already here. Just come watch The People's Court and eat pizza. It'll be really fun!"

And I turned around and slammed the door shut so hard the sound made my ears ring.

So furious. Bright red flashes, fuzzy Christmas lights, swelled in and out of focus, blurring my vision. And before I knew it I was back at the inn and I didn't remember anything about walking, like my body took over while my brain boiled in some kind of rage trance.

I didn't even say hello to Alf when I walked in, just went straight up to my room and slammed the door again because I wanted my ears to keep ringing.

And in there, I pressed and pressed and pressed so hard on the sore spot I thought I could feel grease and blood and sweat seep from my pores like a wet sponge.

And then I started doing something I'd never done before.

I pressed my nail into my scalp and made a half-moon slice, the way you would break into an orange. And I worked at the slice, pulling it up, picking picking picking at it.

I picked and I picked and I picked until under my nail was all crammed up with blood and a glob of it drew a slow, heavy line down my face. ————————

Close-up of blood glob falling over her lip. This is a horror movie, so some of this blood has to be sexy blood. Like this sexy glob.

Fourth Entry

Alf and I spent the bulk of our time standing or sitting around the desk together. Sometimes we'd use the computer but not often. It doesn't have the Internet. Just some really lousy computer card games like Solitaire. And the ancient software we use for checking people in and out of the hotel. Anyway it looks like a computer and has a keyboard and chairs and stuff so we hang out around it anyway. Kinda like how you'll still look at a TV even when it's off.

In case you hadn't noticed, I've started writing in you a lot, diary. Like once I started I just couldn't stop. Even when I want to stop I can't stop. And I'm carrying you with me all the time now, only wearing clothes that you can fit into, like sweaters with big front pockets even though it's hot outside.

In fact I'm writing in you RIIIIGGGGH-HHHT NOOOOW. Ha. Sometimes I write in you at the front desk, like I am riiiigggghhhhht noooow, and other times I take you to this little closet underneath the main staircase. It's a weird shape, kind of a leaning triangle cut out of the wall. There was nothing in it when I found it but a stool and a bare light bulb. Over the bulb I fastened a little red lantern with a little black-haired girl running around it. Almost like a cartoon when I spun it really fast. I found it at a garage sale a million years ago and always knew it'd serve some special purpose one day. Actually not really. But now that it does serve a special purpose, that lie seems true.

I asked Olivia what the closet had been for and she said Holcomb[12] had built it as a "time-out" room for his son. She kept it the way it'd been all those years ago because she thought it would be a kind of attraction to people, to see part of the building in its original state. Instead it mostly got them talking about the punishment. Being forced to sit in a dark room alone for an indefinite amount of time.

---

12 Nathanial Holcomb, a doctor and abolitionist, originally built the estate in 1847.

What if he'd locked his son in and then tripped and fell and hit his head and died? And his poor son was stuck in there to starve to death. Die all alone. Even if someone found him before he starved to death, he'd never be the same. I wonder if it's better to know you'll never be let out of a closet than it is to think that someone, at any moment, might unlock the door and open it and set you free. [13]

At least with a diary you're not really alone.

Maybe it's not exactly fair to call this, you, a diary. Because I don't say, like, Dear Diary, or like, Dear Noelle, and to be honest I don't tell you everything. Not that I lie but I just know I wouldn't tell you EVERYTHING, like for example, if I did something illegal, I probably wouldn't write it down in here because that would be stupid.

Though you do seem to have a way of prying things out of me. What is it about

Possible spin-off movie about Holcomb's son: "He's OUT, he's ANGRY, and he's BURYING PEOPLE ALIVE!" Please forward that essay to me.

13 Holcomb did indeed have a son. He wrote an essay on the subject of sensory depravation, discipline, and punishment using his son as a test subject. It seems from this section that Noelle was aware of the experiment and likely the subsequent essay. Sensory depravation punishment, also known as "white torture," is said to cause the loss of a sense of self and personal identity. After Holcomb died, the essay was found and published as more of a horror story than a scientific document.

you? Is Alf right? Is it just girls who pour things into diaries? Who plant these sticks of dynamite around? Who let you judge them constantly by confessing every little thing?

Anyway maybe I'm mostly using you, diary, on the off-chance I accidentally drop you somewhere or you, like, fall out a car window and some mystery person in a fancy car spots you on the road, stops and picks you up, and reads you and thinks, like, "Wow, what a great writer this Noelle is! This diary, it should be a novel!"

Then the mystery person with the fancy car tracks me down and makes me famous and takes me away from everyone forever. Especially Herman. Who I'm able to douse in my new money so he's quiet forever, my fiery guilt finally smothered.

Actually, maybe you're my surrogate conscience, diary. Like, I'm actually in a mental institution and I'm doing this experimental diary therapy to develop or repair my somehow non-existent or deformed conscience. Writing a fix into my deficient brain. THERE IS NO INN!!! THERE IS NO ALF!!! This diary is a manufactured judge to my terrible thoughts and deeds, and if I don't keep writing in it, don't keep confessing, I might lose my conscience forever, turn into a sociopath and kill everyone … dun dun dun…

That's too exciting.

Probably I'm just a regular old boring narcissist who is, naturally, too vain to appear that way. And that's not exciting at all. This diary is a record of nothing really. Except for how sad it is that this might be the version of my story I'd write to make myself seem great to a stranger.

Which actually probably reveals more about me than even my most honest self ever really could.

I like how some things just have authority because they are what they are. A diary has authority. Truth is implied. Because it's a diary, SEE? But maybe I have to start saying DEAR DIARY for all of it to be considered true. So maybe I'll start:

Dear Diary, my mother[14] *never left and my*

---

14 Many attempts have been made to contact Noelle Dixon's mother, Roberta Eldridge. She currently lives with her second husband, Richard Eldridge, and their two daughters in Swift Current, Saskatchewan. All we really know at this point is she divorced Herman Dixon quickly and quietly, handing over custody of Noelle immediately after she was born and with apparent ease, judging from their lawyers' records. She disappeared completely from their lives after that. Both of Roberta's parents had already died before Noelle was born; however, they too had lived in King City and were considered friendly, though private, members of the community. Herman's parents are also dead.

dad isn't sick and annoying and I stopped picking at my sore spot and all the skin has healed perfectly.

That's stupid.

Actually, diary, isn't it weird that I'd probably hate you if you were real because you're the better version of me?

I wish you were alive. I wish you were alive. I wish you were alive. I wish you were alive. I wish you were alive. I wish you were alive. According to my dad, I just gave birth to you. So you're a real person now. Lying open on the floor, face down, covered in fluids. But I guess more brain fluids as opposed to vag fluids. I wipe you off and I kiss you and now you're totally and completely real. There you go. *You're WELCOME.*

I said, *YOU'RE WELCOME.*

Now you were born *exactly* the same way I was. You're indebted to me always because I wished you to life. YOU HAVE THIS MIRACULOUS GIFT OF LIFE BECAUSE OF MEEEEEEEEEEEEEEE. So massage my weak sphincter with this four-way massager so I can take a solid poop. KIDDING. Ha ha. Except it's not funny at all.

I don't really know what difference it'll make to you to be alive now. Except that maybe I won't bring you into the bathroom anymore. Because that's kinda cruel now that you can breathe.

Wished to life like me. So I love you now and you've gotta love me. Because I'm your mother and your father. You're mine. And you'll be whatever I want you to be.

Fifth Entry

Diary, I don't know how I went the first month [15] of the summer without you. I guess that's my boredom threshold. One month. And after that I start going insane. Insane enough to start writing in a diary.

So far no other scary thing has happened in my room. Just that light on and that door closing. Which really, when I think back on it, wasn't even that scary. It was definitely weird but I didn't feel like, you know, anything was going to pop out and hurt me or whatever.

Maybe it's kind of nice to know that you

---

15 We know Noelle's start date at the inn was June 1st, so this sentence indicates that the first entry in the diary, as well as the incident that took place in her bedroom, occurred in early July.

never have to leave a place if you don't want to. That I could just kill myself here, right now, and haunt the inn forever, kill myself and be away from Herman instead of actually running away, which, really, would be a lot of work. And maybe it's great to be dead here, better than heaven, for so many souls to want to stay.

Become a BUMP IN THE NIGHT.

Diary, you might be what's keeping me safe from the BUMPS IN THE NIGHT. I'm not alone anymore, with you next to me in bed. Maybe if I didn't have you, whatever closed the bathroom door would have snuck out in the middle of the night and sliced open my throat, so fast I'd never know what hit me.

But it's the least you can do, you know, being as I gave you LIFE. Geez.

Sixth Entry

So diary, now that you're alive and you'll be working at the inn here with me, I'll explain how it works: Alfred and I can sleep at night if we want to, but at least one of us has to be "on-call," which means that we keep this light-up buzzer thing in our room that connects to the front door and goes off if someone walks into the foyer. Oh, and the on-call person also has to redirect calls from the front desk to the phone next to their bed in case one of the guests needs something.

Alf and I were no strangers to the stories about the inn, obviously, [16] so for the first

---

16 Not only would Noelle have been aware of the inn's unusual reputation from having grown up in King City, but also library records indicate that Noelle researched its history quite thoroughly before applying for the job.

little while neither of us could sleep. And when the buzzer was in my room I could only stare at it, shallow breaths, just on the edge of screaming, waiting waiting for it to light up and for me to have to go downstairs and find a corpse slouching in the foyer, staring at me with cold dead eyes.

It happened once. Not the corpse with the cold dead eyes, thank god. But once the buzzer buzzed in the middle of the night and I clutched my chest and kicked my legs and screamed at the top of my lungs, blankets flying, and Alf came barging into my room screaming too, "What's wrong what's wrong what's wrong?!" and I pointed at the buzzer and he immediately understood because he felt the same way when it was in his room at night, worried and terrified and just WAIT-ING for it to light up.

So we went downstairs together and found a very old, very thin man in the front foyer who claimed to be speaking at a conference the next day about the effects of a reduced calorie diet on life expectancy. He smelled of wet, wadded towels and when you looked at him straight-on, as we had to from behind the front desk, his hunched shoulders made it look as though his head were a hunting trophy, mounted onto his chest. After we checked him in, we carried his luggage up the stairs and he handed us both pamphlets instead of tips. For the record, the secret to a longer life is not better than money.

Anyway, neither of us could fall asleep again for the rest of the night.

A lot of people say they've seen HIM here. Nathanial Holcomb himself[17] still creeping around THE HAUNTED INN. Previous guests claimed to have seen him standing over their beds at night, slamming their windows shut, passing through their walls, wheezing some cryptic message into their ears right before sleep overcomes them.

Most of our very few guests are here for the novelty. People who have heard the stories and want to see ghosts or experience

He can't be our slasher either. No ghosts. Our slasher has to be flesh and blood so he can kill anywhere, not just the inn. Important for sequels.

---

17 In the late 1980s, two mediums, a physicist, and a parapsychologist were called to do a report on the property and its alleged paranormal activities. In the report, one of the mediums said this: "Nathanial Holcomb is here. Oh, he's here all right. He's the one who pulls the strings. He's in the walls; he's in the windows and the floors. He *is* the house. And he craves misery. He craves tragedy. He'll twist any living person to his will if they give him the chance. All he wants is blood. Burn it to the ground. There will never be peace here."

PARANORMAL PHENOMENA;[18] people who live far enough away from King City to not take it seriously. Because the people in town take it very seriously. Locals always cross the street when they get too near. Apparently the mailman even insisted on having a separate box built at the end of the block so he wouldn't have to set foot on the porch. Olivia[19] hates the mailman now. She

---

18 Interviews with people who have stayed at the inn reveal common complaints of cold spots in the house, areas that just won't get warm no matter how much heat or insulation management applies. Many guests have reported missing eyeglasses, hairbrushes, small personal items that simply reappear in strange places or in places the guests swear they checked. Strange sounds: scratching in the walls, whispering behind closed doors; the "bumps in the night" manager Olivia Grieves mentioned. One particularly disturbed guest claims that she watched her bathroom faucet turn on by itself, piping hot water full blast, and that night she had a vivid dream about someone drowning her, pushing her head into a sink full of blood.

19 Olivia Grieves, manager of the inn for the past twelve years and the second person at the scene of the crime after Jessica West's phone call to the police. Olivia was hired by the great-great-grandniece of Nathanial Holcomb, Miss Anita Fray, who'd inherited the place from her father a few years before. Her father, Alec Fray, had run it when it was an apartment building and knew Margaret Grimley and Margaret's father personally. Anita Fray refused to comment on the recent massacre except to say, "Why do you think I don't go inside?" She's been generous with supplying historical documents on the house, however, and allowed us to copy the quote in footnote 17 from the medium's report.

calls him a superstitious fool and won't even say hi to him when she sees him in town.

You can imagine what she thinks of our novelty guests.

But anyway, I think a lot of people lie. About seeing stuff here. Not that stuff doesn't happen, obviously it does, but I don't think so many guests are seeing it.

Or maybe they're not lying but they want so bad to have actually seen something that they make themselves see something.

Because to me it actually feels like the house is at its MOST quiet on those nights when we have novelty visitors staying. Conspicuously quiet. As though whatever or whoever makes "bumps in the night" is spiteful and funny and doesn't want to give anyone the satisfaction. At least that's what I tell myself when I've been really scared of seeing something. That like, wanting to see something, or even just pretending you do, means you probably won't.

We've got a lot of stupid rules like that. Stuff we've made up to protect ourselves because we're scared and can never really know what the hell is going on here. For example, Alf and I flick the basement light on and off five times before we leave it on, so that the ghosts know that they can't pop out if they wanna be seen. Because that's just rude. Because we've warned them, told them we're coming, given them plenty of time to set themselves up in a non-terrifying way if they really want to be seen.

We've even gone as far as to write these things down and tack them up behind the desk where guests can't see. [20]

We add to the rules as we go.

"Bumps in the night." That's how Olivia always puts it. "There are bumps in the night here and don't you go looking for them."

Olivia told us that she used to work the nightshift all alone.

Most of her life she'd been on one night-shift or another. Gas stations and grocery

---

20 Rules, copied from the paper behind the desk:
  1. All lights must be flicked on and off five
     times before being turned totally on.
     When the lights are on they can't come out.
  2. Tell yourself you want to see a ghost if
     you really DON'T want to see a ghost.
  3. Never close the medicine cabinet mirror
     while looking into it—something terrible
     WILL be standing behind you.
  4. Don't antagonize the ghosts.
  5. Don't unlock locked doors.
  6. If you hear a weird sound run away.
     And don't run upstairs somewhere if
     running out the front door is an option.
  7. RUN up and down all staircases.
  8. Don't, under any circumstances, go
     down ANY of the basement hallways.

stores, one of those sharp older cashier ladies who've seen it all, but not in the way that she's always trying to give you advice or butt into your business, because she's seen it all so she knows how annoying that is. She was just a regular person who'd conditioned herself to an alternative circadian clock. But now she couldn't work nightshifts anymore. She wouldn't stay at the inn after dark. She'd had a nightmare, she said. And the doctor told her she should be home at night from now on.

We were scared and everything but both Alf and I, on some level, really want to see something.

Alf because of his sister. He said that instead of being scared it would make him happy to know that she hadn't just disappeared into nothing after she flailed to death.

And me, I don't know why. I guess just because it would be exciting.

And Olivia's "nightmare" wasn't really a "nightmare." That's just what she started calling it after the doctor got involved and told her IT MUST HAVE BEEN A NIGHTMARE.

She told us that before the doctor came and pulled her off the nightshift, she was positive that the nightmare was real. That

Wink[21] was stripping off long ribbons of her flesh and sucking them up like spaghetti. And the pain was real and his cold hands were real and she could hear it, her skin stretched to snapping, the grip of her flesh on her bones coming loose.

Not that either Alf or I want something like that to happen to us. But something, yeah. Like, something more than what happened to me in my bedroom. That was creepy and everything, but now when I think back on it I'm not even sure it really happened, because maybe I was tired and maybe it was a dream. And if I hadn't written it all down in you, diary, maybe I would have forgotten it completely by now.

But Alf hasn't seen anything yet, or maybe he has but he's forgotten because he isn't writing anything down in his JOURNAL.

Alf is a little bit older than me. So, like a diary has implied authority, Alf has implied authority. Which is really annoying.

We're at the front desk now. It's long and wide and made of wood, with lots of cupboards underneath, some locked and some open, filled with printer paper and a pathetic

---

21 Margaret Grimley's boyfriend; died in the suite in 1979, the result of consuming infected human flesh.

lost-and-found box. We each have our own rolling chair and we take turns standing when Olivia's around and needs one too.

The desk looks out over the lobby: a piano with a long bench, six strange armless chairs, a tall fireplace surrounded by antique pokers and brushes, all of it collecting dust that Alf and I are supposed to clean off daily but don't. The main floor is totally carpeted so footsteps are fresh-snow quiet. It's orange and brown and I'd love to drift into its patterned space but I don't wanna put my face on the floor.

The lighting is sort of weird here, a stretch of too-bright bulbs running above our desk so that everything else looks too dark by comparison.

Alf and I are both sitting in our chairs here. We have one guest upstairs. A woman who wore a long black coat and carried her few belongings in a cloaked birdcage. When Alf reached for it to carry it up for her she pulled it away from him, startled, and said, "I can do it myself, young man," and eyed him up and down like he was a criminal. Poor Alf. She was in the city to attend her great-grandniece's baptism. She seemed like the kind of relative who was only invited to the really boring stuff.

Anyway, we're both sitting in our chairs at the front desk and I'm writing in here and Alf is playing Solitaire and he just said, "Noelle, did you ever notice that there are two 'I's in solitaire? Isn't that weird? Like, it seems kind of deliberate, doesn't it? Considering what the word means?"

"Geez, Alf, I think you're really onto something."

"Well, it is kinda weird, isn't it? It doesn't take two 'I's to play Solitaire. Get it?"

"Oh, I get it alright. You better watch your back, man. Information like that has a way of placing people in shallow graves."

"Goddamit, Noelle, I'm just making an observation."

"Tell me, what are you observing right now, in my face?"

"You think what I just said is the most insightful thing you've ever heard."

And I rolled my eyes and Alfred told me I rolled my eyes like a sixteen-year-old and I called him a pervert. He really doesn't like when I call him a pervert lately. I think because he feels like kind of a pervert for having a crush on me, even though he's only a year older than me and I'm not a virgin and he is.

That's actually a good example of why Alf

having a crush on me is annoying. Suddenly I can't call him a pervert anymore. I used to do this impression of him before, Alfred the Virgin Pervert, where he's this sicko who's got these really foul perversions but they never get far because he blows his load too soon, being a virgin and all. So like, I do this voice all low and breathy and pervy and say something like, "Then I show the child the candy and the child reaches for it and uuuuuugh god, oh yes oh yes yes yes!" and Alf the Virgin Pervert ejaculates everywhere. And we used to laugh really hard. But now all of a sudden, Alf doesn't wanna be made fun of for being a virgin. Or a pervert.

I wonder what his expectations are for when he finally has sex.

Actually I think I know. He wants it to feel like when you hug someone so hard, so hard you just want them to burst because only that bursting will show them how much you love them, and that's what Alf thinks sex will be like, actually making that person you love burst, really showing them how you feel, bursting together even, so that every new surface area of every burst bit can touch, touching like never ever before.

That's what Alf wants.

That's how Alf started acting when he got

the crush. It's how I knew. Like he wanted to make me burst. Which maybe means he loves me? I don't know. I just wish he'd stop. It stresses me out to think that this, our being friends, could be ruined somehow.

I've been picking at my scalp all morning. I just can't seem to stop now that I've started. I promise myself that each little hunk I dig out will be the last. Then it's not. Then I'm bleeding and it looks terrible and I've gotta hide it under my hair with a ponytail.

This is the first time in my life I'm happy I've got brown hair.

Olivia is outside smoking right now. She's wearing a short-sleeved shirt today. I know this sounds terrible, but I really wish she wouldn't expose us to her body. Her arms look like overcooked chicken wings, a thin, dry membrane connecting her forearm to her biceps. When something as fucked-up-looking as Olivia's arms peek out from beneath clothes it's hard not to imagine what her fucked-up naked body must look like.

Then it's really hard to stop.

I see braided ligaments beneath tinted saran wrap.

Alf said it probably looks like someone stuck a vacuum hose up her butt and sucked everything soft out.

I never want to get old. You can't even wear a ponytail when you get old. Olivia wears one and it makes her look strange and creepy before you get to know her and realize that she's not.

I said that out loud once, that I never want to get old, and Alf said, "I think you'll be a good-looking old lady."

See, if he were just my friend he'd never say anything like that. If he were just my friend he'd call me a hag. That's another good example of why Alf's crush is annoying.

Anyway. Olivia. Poor old Olivia. Slowly thawing to daytime life. Almost like a mitten lost in autumn, snowed on and frozen stiff through winter, revealed soaking wet and twisted up in summer.

The only parts of Olivia that simply refuse to thaw are the first two fingers of her left hand; she keeps them clawed and erect and applies pressure to an imaginary cigarette that becomes real on the front porch every fifteen minutes. You can almost see a meter above her head, like a thermometer but not for temperature, getting higher and higher and her getting bitchier and bitchier the longer she spends inside with an empty claw and at 15 minutes the meter spews from the top and she'll power-walk to the porch to reset.

You should see the way she smokes.

Deep drags. Much deeper than her regular wheezy breathing. It's funny how a smoker like Olivia can only take deep breaths when it's cigarette smoke they're inhaling, regular air being too thin and boring. Regular air makes her cough and spit and wretch. She can't laugh in regular air.

On windless nights she'll release big smoky mouthfuls, then gobble them back up again fast. Almost teasing them: You'll never escape, you must pleasure my lungs again and again until you're NOTHING!

"Double the value," she once said of her unique smoking method.

And then she tried to laugh regular air and coughed. Or maybe she didn't actually cough but it just seemed like she should have. Let's just say she coughed, because it's better that way.

It's hard to imagine that Olivia was ever someone's daughter. A fresh little baby all soft and new and warm.

There are five cats that come and go as they please around here, in and out through a basement window Olivia insists we keep open all the time, even when it's raining outside.

Olivia says that they keep the rat problem in check but really she just loves them and wants them around. Sometimes when she sits outside in her chair on the porch she'll take her shoes off and let them lick and nibble at the dried skin peeling off her feet. Her tissue face twisted: tickled, delighted.

Other times she lays her head over the back of the chair, skin fallen in slow globs, pooling under, away from her skull, so you can see up close just how near the elderly really are to death.

Pinched shut eyes and that vacant mouth. Olivia's mouth so dark inside and crisp around the edges it looks burned into her tissue face with one of her cigarettes.

An old woman, sleeping or dead. The cats licking and nibbling away at her feet. Maybe they don't know either if she's sleeping or dead. What difference would it make to them? I always hope it's neither. That poor Olivia goes into her own patterned space somehow, not sleeping, not dead, but somewhere in between.

Because their purpose is to catch rats, Olivia thinks it's very clever to call the cats the Rat Pack, and she even named them accordingly: Frank, Dean, Sammy, Peter, and Joey. Though I think Sammy, Peter, and

Joey are actually girls. I haven't checked or anything, they just seem to have girl faces.

Sometimes at night I peek in on them from the top of the basement steps. The moonlight pouring in through the window makes their backs look slick and oily and they move around each other like piranhas in a tank.

But they're otherwise very nice cats.

Alf and I had a big favor to ask Olivia. He'd been nagging me for days to please, please, pleeeeeeease do the asking.

"Pleeeeeeease Noelle," he begged. "I can't ask her this. I can't. Those eyebrows. I won't be able to gauge her reaction, I'll play the situation all wrong."

For whatever reason, Olivia didn't have any eyebrows. Based on two overly active mounds of flesh above her eyes, she guessed where her eyebrows should be and drew new ones on each morning. Because of this Alf found it very difficult to speak with her face to face. He couldn't tell if she was mad or sad or happy and he found it unsettling.

I'd seen this disability of Alf's in action before. He turned into a complete idiot when he spoke to Olivia, but a weird kind of idiot. Not stupid. Just totally unpredictable. Like once she asked him to rake the leaves and handed him a rake from the closet, and he grazed his pinky finger against hers very purposefully and awkwardly and afterwards couldn't understand or explain why. He said that her face made him think it was the right thing to do so he did it.

When I couldn't stop laughing at him, he got mad and said, "Do you think I don't already wanna kill myself, Noelle?" And, "You don't understand. It's like talking to someone in a mask," all seriously, when the laughing got truly out of control.

So anyway that's why Alf had to be the lookout, watching her smoke on the porch from an upstairs window of the inn while I waited downstairs to sort of stop her in the hall like I was on my way to do something else.

As soon as I heard his feet stomping, our signal, I ran from the front desk to the bathroom, where I waited till I heard the back door open, then shut, and then I flushed the toilet to add authenticity to our ruse and emerged into the hallway and cut her off.

"Oh hi, Noelle!" said Olivia, all full of happy smoke.

"Hi Olivia," I replied. "Pretty nice weather, right? Must feel good to be able to smoke outside again without the Big Jacket."

We all shared the Big Jacket for outside

duties. Sometimes Olivia would leave ancient-looking candies in the pockets. Alf and I didn't know if they were supposed to be presents for us or if she was saving them for later. Either way, we often ate them.

"You betcha," she said, and she WINKED at me. Which meant that I really had to ask right now in this second of her perfect smoky happiness.

"Olivia, can I ask you a favor?"

"Okay," and the meter suddenly shot up. Favors. No one likes favors.

"Okay, so Alf and I, like, we were wondering if we could, if no one came to stay at the inn of course, we were wondering if we could invite some of our friends over for the Anniversary, and have, like, just a little dinner here."

"The Anniversary?" I saw the meter shoot up faster still.

"You know. Just, we're here every night all summer. We just want to hang out with our friends, and—"

Olivia felt particularly guilty about "us kids" spending all of our summer nights in this "wretched place" so I knew it was the right thing to say.

"Godammit, Noelle, I don't want you thinking about all that grim stuff. And more importantly I don't want this goddamn town to keep thinking about that grim stuff for fuck's sake—oh cripes, sorry, Noelle, pardon the swears."

"Oh, yeah, no problem."

"Okay, well, alright. If absolutely no guests show up, sure, you guys can have a few people over but really keep it quiet, alright, Noelle? I'm so tired of that story I could spit."

Then she walked right back outside for another cigarette because agreeing to the favor had depleted her meter too fast. Alf stomped-stomped-stomped happily on the floor above.

Seventh Entry

I guess, diary, now that you're alive, you'll wanna know all about the Anniversary.

Alf and I are working at the very place the celebrated incident took place, so it's kind of our responsibility to have a massive party.

Kids in this town had been having Anniversary Parties since before Alf and I were born. There aren't any tattoo parlours here, or seedy bars, or even drug dealers who can get anything harder than pot. So celebrating the most horrific bit of town history is really one of the only ways for us to rebel. Mothers say it's sick. Fathers say it's disrespectful. That's about the best we can hope for. Force them all to remember what they want to forget.

Okay, so The Boy Eats Girl Inn is actually really old. I'm not sure exactly how old, but I do know that we tell people about Oscar Wilde[22] staying here, back when it was one family's giant home. And about how the basement had been part of the Underground Railroad.[23] So however old that would make it, that's how old it is.

It's kinda sad when you think about it, that this great old house, a house that's seen it all, now has a buzzing honeymoon-red sign on it. And to a pair of kids like Alf and me it may as well be a Wal-Mart or a McDonalds or some other shitty summer job. Old buildings should really get the same kind of respect that old trees do, but that just doesn't happen. I guess because trees are more technically "alive" and often people in towns have no reason to wanna forget about particular trees like they do particular buildings.

So, back in the '70s or the '80s or some-thing, I forget exactly when, The Boy Eats Girl

— *Begin flash-back with Noelle voiceover, then let the flashback take over.*

22 There is no evidence to support this claim.

23 Holcomb, a vocal abolition activist, constructed the basement to have hiding spots, camouflaged doors with powerful locks, a kitchen area, bedrooms, and even a bathroom. It was also as soundproof as was humanly possible during that time, all safeguards to help secretly hide slaves along their paths to freedom.

Inn was, for a brief time, a very fancy apartment building.[24] The same half-moon windows and red brick and white shutters on the outside, but inside, beneath all the bad carpet we've got now, swirling marble floors and dark hardwood and real art on the walls. There was an even bigger piano in the lobby, with someone on the bench playing it all the time, and a harp with a long-necked lady harpist, and a doorman in a suit with tasseled epaulets.

A very overweight woman named Margaret Grimley was kept in the biggest apartment in the building by her wealthy father and his trophy wife. She had the suite. The whole top floor of the building. As far away from her family's home as possible. They visited very rarely and paid every bill without question, even when she pushed it for attention. Like ordering masseuses to the room and demanding that buttery dinners be delivered right to her door on a special rolling cart and tray (which they'd also had to buy).

She was the product of her father's first marriage, to a dark-haired woman who was

---

24 From 1976 to 1985 it served as an apartment building.

dead now. Killed herself shortly after Margaret was born. [25]

Margaret trolled lonely hearts ads and missed connections in the daily paper endlessly. Looking even just for friends. The doorman was constantly seeing people in and out of the building on her behalf, so often, in fact, that he eventually stopped bothering to have them write their names down, just asking which room they were headed to. "The suite" was almost always the reply.

At first he'd brought it up to the woman's father, but the popular theory is that Mr. Grimley greased the doorman's palms to keep him quiet.

Chances are her father hoped that one of the visitors would end up murdering her. It would be cheaper in the long run.

Finally she met someone special. A man from somewhere down south. And her father

---

25 Edna Grimley, Margaret's mother. She was a sullen woman, and overweight like Margaret. Apparently she spoke often of suicide even before Margaret was born. She hung herself in an upstairs closet of the family home using a low, sturdy cupboard and thick nylon. Legs purple and bent at the knee, feet black and dragging on the ground. It is a common misconception that the body's unconscious will to survive will take over when a person is attempting to self-destruct.

and his trophy wife let her keep him in the suite. His name was Wink, and that was that, and if they wanted to ask him any more questions he'd cut their fucking tongues out. He had a large indented scar down the front of his head, a hook that just snared his wormlike eyebrow. He said he'd taken a bad fall and hit his head in prison, where he'd roomed with an old devil who'd taught him magic. [26]

Of course Margaret had never really been one to leave the apartment, always ordering everything right to her door anyway,

---

26 In Wink's diaries, he claims that his roommate in prison, the devil he lived with, was the son of Nathanial Holcomb—the same child who'd been locked in a closet and studied in Nathanial's essay on sensory deprivation and discipline. According to Wink's journals, Nathanial's son called himself Sal (short for Hansel, which was indeed the Holcomb child's name), and Sal predicted that after Wink got out of jail, he would move to King City and answer a very special lonely hearts ad in the paper; Sal told him he'd move into a swanky apartment with an enormous woman, and that if that much came true, then it was Wink's responsibility to trap sick and sad people in the suite and murder them. Sal promised Wink that the house would make it worth his while; that the house "never forgot the kindness of those who fed it." Wink said in his journals that he would do all the murders again and much worse if Sal had asked him to; from the tone of his writing, it's obvious that Wink truly believed Sal was a devil. However, there's an odd discrepancy in Wink's account. In the late 1960s and early 1970s, when Wink served his prison time, Sal Holcomb would have been well over 100 years old.

but now Wink answered the door instead, Margaret just a pair of pudgy, red-toenailed feet hanging over the bed, lobbing buoyant hellos over Wink's head to whoever had the depressing misfortune of knocking.

That she was totally preoccupied with Wink was a relief to her father and his trophy wife who just wanted to get on with their lives and their money. They overlooked anything that might have disturbed them about the strapping young gentleman who'd fallen head over heels for their only daughter, moved right in, and stood in the doorway between Margaret and the world.

After a little while, Margaret and Wink started browsing the lonely hearts ads again, together, looking for women to invite over so that Wink could have sex with them and Margaret could watch, or at least that's what it said in Wink's journals. And again the doorman stopped taking names, stopped noticing the comings and goings altogether while his pockets grew fatter and fatter with Margaret's father's cash.

That's why it was hard to track down when the women first started going missing.

But they did go missing. And kept going missing. Because together, in that apartment, Wink and Margaret murdered and kept them. Fifteen women in total. Way up high, a floor all their own.

During this time Margaret became pregnant. And doubly unfortunate for her, Wink had fallen in love with their last captive. He'd decided with his new lover to kill Margaret. And he explained in his journals that he had to do it very slowly. Because the old devil he'd roomed with in prison, the devil he claimed was Nathanial Holcomb's poor, sensory-deprived son, taught him that all lovers must be killed as slowly as possible.

He strapped Margaret to the bed, not that she could have easily gotten up anyway being as big as she was, and over time severed each of her limbs with care, one by one, tying them off tight as sausage ends, stopping the blood off so she would remain alive. And he ate her.

Eventually her wounds pulsated with infection. Wink got sick from consuming so much soft raw flesh.

The police found hundreds of journals about how he'd done it, what each little bit of her tasted like, about how he hated her so much by then that all of her tasted delicious because it meant she was suffering. One line I remember from the paper was, "How cum she never tastid this good wen I luved her?"

I thought that was kind of beautiful in a way.

As for the baby, it'd been a boy. And he ate him first. [27]

And the captive he loved, he believed she loved him too. So, after she proved her loyalty by eating a slice of by that time already very infected Margaret meat, he let her leave. Alone. To get a change of clothes and all her money and valuables so they could disappear. But of course, after a seemingly endless stream of vomit and a short faint in an alley, she went to the police and that was that.

So anyway that's why it kind of makes sense that this place is called The Boy Eats Girl Inn sometimes. When the M is on the fritz.

And that's the Anniversary we'll be celebrating. The Anniversary of Margaret's death.

Alf and I invited everyone from school. Literally everyone. Because basically if we didn't,

Are you kidding me? Tell me you found this kid. Please. If not, that's priority one. Find him, get him to sign off, make him our flesh and blood slasher.

---

27 Story mostly confirmed. Some of the details were invented, however, either by Noelle or warped over years by the imperfect whispers of town lore. The baby wasn't eaten, but had in fact been born a few weeks before they murdered their first victim. According to his journals, Wink wanted to kill the baby, but Margaret convinced him to allow her stepmother to quietly adopt it instead. After the murders, Margaret's father and stepmother moved to another state. Their current whereabouts, as well as the child's, are unknown.

they would all hate us and I wouldn't blame them. We're sort of obligated, like I said.

June and Andrea will be coming. They're my two sort-of-closest girlfriends. But more so, the three of us are just there. Leftovers. Who probably all prefer the idea of not being alone to each other's actual company. But I guess that's kinda bitchy. I do like them too. I don't know. I've barely seen them all summer.

I guess people at school would say that we're best friends. Because that's the high school phrase for what we look like: BEST FRIENDS. June and Andrea and I are THE BEST FRIENDS and Alf is some guy who wears turtlenecks and has a weird haircut who happens to have a crush on me.

June and Andrea are cool though. They are. Because they're kind of bad. They like to get drunk and smoke pot and skip class and hang out late and do whatever they feel like. And they're smart too but not in a boring way. Like, they don't study or get good grades or anything but they're funny and they know what's cool and they know just exactly how to watch TV and talk at the same time. You know how some people just aren't good at that? They talk at all the wrong times and when they do talk they don't get it, it's not funny in the right way. Anyway I guess it's the kind of thing that's hard to explain, but June and Andrea, they're great to watch TV with. Even commercials. Great to get drunk with and great to be hungover with, watching TV and eating.

Alf's got this one friend named Ian that he hangs out with at school. Ian smells sort of bad and I think there's something wrong with his feet, they both turn inward a bit so he's always rubbing holes into the knees of his jeans and his mom has to patch them, but he's nice enough. He'll probably show up too.

I can't wait for the Anniversary.

Eighth Entry

Big clump of hair in my hand, an island of bloody scalp hanging from the end. I want to eat it. I want it to be squishy, pudding soft, so I can bite right through it. But I won't. Cuz it won't be squishy pudding soft, it'll be chewy and grainy and juicy. Overripe even though it's just fresh off of someone. Me. Just do it Noelle, just eat it up because then you're closer. Closer to the spot. You'll get there, you can soothe it right up close. Touch it Noelle. You can touch it.

> *Keep digging.*
> *Don't stop.*
> *You'll get there.*
> *Keep digging.*

There's a tool down here. A big sharp tool I could use to dig. I wanna wind up, let the weight of the tool in my hands move my arms in big walloping circles, then let it land THUD heavy in my head, pierce through my skull, right into the sore spot. God yes, yes, yes. But I can't. It's too heavy for me right now. I've gotta get stronger still.

Here kitty kitty kitty. Kitty kitty kitty. I've got a treat for you. Flesh-eating piranha kitty.

Maybe one of the piranhas will eat it. One of the flesh-eating piranhas. Swimming around down here, rubbing up against each other all night.

I got one. I got a piranha. It was easy. It trusts me. It wants to be fed the meat, the island of flesh. I put it in his face but he doesn't want it anymore, I smush it up into his mouth and some gets in his nose and he sneezes and tries to get away. Sammy. But I've got him I've got him and he can't get out and he's kinda scratching at me but he doesn't have any claws because he got away from someone's home, someone who took his claws away when he was small, and he's since been depending on just his charm and good looks to get by in the mean streets.

I have him squished under one arm, dragging the big tool behind me in the other. He tries to fight as I take him down the dark hallway.

The more he fights the harder I press down on him.

Then we are in the room. Whispering whispering whispering outside and even inside and sometimes it sounds like it's right in my ear, warm whispers tickling, filling my ear with real wet heat, then an icy finger fast and hard, bypassing my skull, penetrating the sore spot, so cold and soothing. I just want to lie here and feel that finger all night so cold and good.

But I can't lie here all night. It urges me to feed the piranha.

I have my knees on Sammy, both of them, hurting him I can tell, because he cries out. One hand claws around his little body like a harness, holding him down. I use my thumb to try to open his mouth and shove the meat in but he won't eat, he won't listen, he won't listen to me. BAD BAD BAD BAD BAD. EAT IT. EAT! EAT IT! YOU MUST EAT IT!!!!!!!!!!!!!!!!!!!!

But he won't. What kind of flesh-eating piranha doesn't want any meat?

So I smash part of his head in with a can of deck stain. Kind of smash and smear so his eyeball pops like a paintball and leaves a streak of blood and guts and color along the floor. His mouth opens easily after that. He eats it up. Eats it right up. Kill the greasy oily piranha. Oh piranha why wouldn't you eat it on your own?

The piranha's not dead though. He's alive but not really. Somewhere in between. This lucky little cat piranha is in patterned space

*and I put him there. And I'm glad too because
he was always such a good cat and All Good
Cats Go To Patterned Space.*

*I get the tool and drag it over to the kitty
kitty kitty. I think about spearing him with
the big tool's sharp end. Imagine it THUNK
through his soft warmth. What do you call this
thing? This thing that goes THUNK through
living softness.*

*I make a move to kill him but something
stops me. An icy white hand, the same cold fingers that'd been in my head, now on my wrist
and whispering whispering whispering that
says if I kill the kitty I'm fucking dead fucking
meat. I'm dead meat and she's going to eat me.
So don't fucking do it.*

Who are you?

Who are you?

*Put it back, the whispering whispers whis-
pers whispers put it back. Put it back Noelle.
It's not time yet. Put it back. So I do.* [28]

---

28 It should be noted that in the original diary, this
    section takes up over twelve pages. It's written in big,
    wide scrawl, recognizable as Noelle's in some ways, but
    also very different from her regular handwriting. At
    the request of our hired parapsychologist, the forensic
    document examiner has located handwriting samples
    from Margaret Grimley, Nathanial Holcomb, and Wink
    and she's comparing them with this version of Noelle's
    handwriting. To what end, I'm not entirely sure.

Ninth Entry

Um. Hi, diary. Yeah. Hi. Um. Just a quick question, ahhhhh what the fuck was that? What the fuck was it? What the hell?

Did that happen? I don't understand. I don't remember writing it. All I remember is going to bed, falling asleep at some point I guess. Then I woke up this morning, brought you into the bathroom (sorry), and found all this crazy stuff inside you.

That stuff is fucking weird. It's really fucking weird. What the fuck is it, diary? Don't show me stuff like that you dick, if you can't explain what the hell it is. Don't make me read it.

Or … write it I guess. Did I write that? It doesn't look like me, it doesn't sound like me. Why did you make me write that? Did

you make me do that? Did you? You cat-hat-
ing bitch diary?

Okay. Did that happen? Did that happen
for real?

Diary, you've gotta tell me honestly if
that happened. If I did that. Now that you're
alive and I'm your mother and your father
you've gotta tell me the truth all the time.
Did that happen last night? Did I do that to
Sammy? Jesus christ I feel sick. I really do. I
wanna rip those pages out of you but I don't
wanna hurt you, diary. Don't show me that
stuff again or I'll have to hurt you. I won't
want to, but you'll have made me, do you
understand?

Okay let me think.

The very very very last thing I remember from last night was lying on my blanket,
drifting off into patterned space, and I guess
just falling asleep that way. Which is odd
actually.

Because I can't fall asleep in patterned
space.

Usually something pulls me out before
I'm even close to sleep.

But I guess last night I did? I must have?
Because it's all I remember.

It used to be I would have found the idea
of falling asleep in patterned space amazing.

It would have been a dream come true. But right now it doesn't feel like a dream come true. Right now it feels like bad things happen in patterned space when you fall asleep in it. And if you've got a diary to write it all down in, then you've gotta read about it.

Diary, you're the only true account. Because you weren't asleep when all that was happening because you don't sleep. You're just as conscious all night long as you are now. Are those pages true? DID THAT REALLY HAPPEN? YOU FUCKING TELL ME YOU BITCH! You just want me to feel bad. You had me write that stuff down so you could judge me. So I could judge me. Quit building a judge into my brain, I don't want it. I don't wanna judge myself this way. Maybe if you were a JOURNAL you wouldn't be such a bitch.

Because maybe this is why little girls have diaries, to build the brain judge, start policing ourselves early because there are a lot more rules for girls than boys. A lot more rules for DIARIES than there are for JOURNALS. Diaries have to start with DEAR DIARY, and they have to contain deep dark secrets, and they have to be kept private. Diaries are worst enemies disguised as best friends. You make us write in you,

you make us tell you everything, then you TURN ON US.

I'm sorry. It's not you.

My head is throbbing.

It must have been Alfred. Diary, was it Alfred? Did Alfred get in and write in you? That stupid fucking jerk. Is this some kind of weird prank? I hope you're reading this right now Alfred, you fucking asshole stupid jerk-face bitch writing that fucked-up shit in my private fucking diary type thing, Alfred you DICK. You stupid tippy-toe butler bastard!

But I know it wasn't Alfred. Alfred would never open my diary. I could leave it anywhere and I know he would never look. That's why I can write such terrible things about him in here. Because he's such a good person.

If Alf used his JOURNAL I know I'd look inside. Because I'm such a bad person. I kill fucking cats apparently for god's sake. Doesn't get much worse than that.

Okay, okay, okay.

It was me who wrote those pages, definitely and absolutely. I do recognize my handwriting in there, sort of, even though it's kind of fucked-up looking. And I'd never told Alf about patterned space before because uhhh I'm not SO fucking psycho that I'd tell someone about that psycho-ass shit.

Whispering. Whispering. Was that the same whispering I heard in my bathroom that night? What was it telling me? Was it telling me to start writing in you? Because I did after that. I obeyed. I started writing and now I can't stop. Goddamn you, diary. What are you? Are you a ghost too?

Okay okay I'm sorry. That's stupid, I know. I'm sorry I keep blaming you. This isn't your fault.

There was a dark concentration of blood all over my pillow this morning. Black under my nails. Dried blood. My blood. I think. Or maybe Sammy's. A section of hair missing. Island of flesh. Jesus. That island of flesh came from my fucking head. It's a proper gouge now, a tiny canyon on my scalp with jagged cliffs. I pressed into it hard, my finger in deep, and it felt good.

Okay, diary, I promise I won't touch it again today. Really. I'm going to try to leave it alone.

It's sore. It's so sore I don't even wanna look at it yet. It hurt to put up my ponytail but I had to have it up to cover the spot.

I'm scared.

My dad was already awake when I came

home. He'd heard me close the front door downstairs and hollered at me from his room.

I found him on his small, messy bed, sitting up with the tray of Q-tips pulled out of the big blue box next to him. His legs crossed under the blankets. He patted his lap.

So I got on the bed and laid my head in the blanket hammock over his lap.

Real Q-tips, not generic "cotton swabs." Even though we're poor he always buys the good ones because he knows I love this.

I told him when I was little that I wanted him to clean my ears forever and he always has and he's never made me feel weird about liking it as much as I do. And he loves it too. Because this is really the only thing he gets to do for me now, the only thing he really can do. He gets to touch me and be close to me like he was once a long time ago when I was a baby and couldn't do anything for myself. I still love this even though I hate him.

Now you know, diary. It's fucking weird, right? Fuck. Writing it down feels weird. Whatever. Don't judge the person who gave birth to you. If I'm weird you're weird too.

He made teeth of his fingers and combed the hair off my face, away from my ears, making himself a nice clean area to rest his arms without leaning on my hair, pulling it so I yell at him.

And then he started digging. And it felt so good. Sort of loud and ticklish and kind of painful. Or, not really painful, but kind of wrong. Like I was tempting permanent ear damage. Tracing the cotton swab in and around the spirals and caverns and folds of my ears. Sometimes the feeling made me shiver and he'd press down on my cheek with his fingertips and say, "Stop that, I don't wanna stab your brain."

He would never stab my brain.

The TV was on in his bedroom, low volume and bright colors flashing just right in the not quite dark. The Home Shopping Channel. A woman with big dark hair talking about an AMAZING BLENDER. It makes ice cream, soup, smoothies, lattes, pasta sauce, dips, etc, etc, etc, etc, etc, etc. The list has to go on for at least an hour. Herman has already bought this blender, a tower on our kitchen counter, so tall, wider at the top like a sarcophagus and thick with dust. He once even phoned in during one of the on-air call-in segments to gush about how great it was, what a healthy lifestyle he was living now, now that he could make smoothies in the morning before work. How he made his daughter healthy sorbets for dessert at night and, oh heck, I make them for me too! Gotta treat yourself, right? He was so personable on the phone. So different. And when he hung up he slumped even more in his chair.

I stared at the TV. At the UNITS SOLD counter slowly increasing.

Early morning light seeping slow and dough-like through the pulled-shut-but-no-longer-effective blinds.

This was the perfect light, the perfect volume on the TV, the perfect ear pleasure to fall asleep to. But then he ruined it. He started talking.

"How was work, sweetie?" He lifted the Q-tip out of my ear so I could hear him. Which made me very angry.

"It was fine."

"Anything weird happen again?"

"What do you mean?"

"You know. What did Olivia call it? Bumps in the night?"

"Oh, that. No, not really. I guess, there's been a lot of weird noises. Definitely some of those cold spots we've heard about. But I haven't seen anything, like a ghost or anything, if that's what you're asking."

Oh, um, I did kill a fucking cat though. Maybe. Yeah, and tried to feed it part of my head. Sooo.

And oh yeah, maybe a ghost told me to do it. Or told me not to do it. I don't really know yet.

It was a giant mistake to tell him about the first weird thing that happened at the inn. The bathroom thing. He had a thousand theories as to what it might have been. He retold it over and over again to Dr. Schiller's other patients on the phone. He'd fret about it every time I left for work, he called me late at night now sometimes to make sure I was okay alone in my room.

I wouldn't be sharing any more close encounters with Herman.

"It worries me, you know," he said. As though I hadn't already heard that a thousand times before.

"I do know."

"If anything happened to my baby, I'd die."

"I know, Dad."

And I squirmed my head a little, to indicate that he should keep cleaning. So he stuck it in again. The Q-tip dangerously deep, thunderously loud, my neck pulled into my body, smile spreading slowly across my face like a dog scratched in just the right spot. He dug and dug, not noticing.

"There should be some kind of drill for you guys to do, like, if something happens again like last time." I could barely hear him over the scraping.

"Like a fire drill?" I whispered, the low volume of my voice a hint for him to stop talking.

"Yeah! Like that. You should draw one up. I'll draw it up for you. Or actually, I'll tell you what to draw and you draw it. My carpal tunnel has been acting up lately."

"Right, your carpal tunnel."

"You know, sarcasm doesn't help."

"It's just weird to me that you should be suffering from a working person's disease."

"Ha ha."

"Now who's being sarcastic?"

"Keep still." And he pressed his warm fingers into my cheek. "Didn't anyone ever teach you not to antagonize a person working in your ear?"

"Well, you would have been the person who failed to teach me that."

"Okay, I'm teaching you now."

I gestured at the TV and said, "Look, it's your blender."

"I know!"

"You make a smoothie today?"

"Don't be smart, Noelle."

"I'm just asking. Say, wanna go to the kitchen and whip us up some homemade soup in minutes?"

"You know, it's not fair."

"What's not fair?"

"These commercials, they're very manipulative, you know. They tell us, you know, we can only live once, so we better eat and drink everything we want, buy everything we want, you know, always get yourself a chicken from Ollie's if you want one because you only live once. And then the next commercial tells us we're all fat and unhealthy so we've gotta buy blenders to make the smoothies. It makes my head hurt. I mean, I guess that's the idea. You buy stuff to make your head stop hurting for a while."

"Well here's another idea, Herman. Stop watching the goddamn shopping channel."

"I can't."

"Here, it's easy."

I grabbed the remote and changed the channel. A talk show. About a woman who'd been ripped apart by her two dogs.

"Cripes!" And I went to change it again.

But Herman said, "Leave it!"

"Why?"

"I don't know. I guess ... maybe it's nice to see people worse off than me."

And he laughed, but I know he was trying to make me feel bad for him.

And then he dug into the top curve of my ear and dragged the Q-tip along it. This was my absolute favorite and I made a loooooooooooooong sound because I couldn't even help it.

"Did that feel good honey?" he asked, smiling.

I nodded.

"Don't nod."

So I stayed still. And watched the show. And I fell asleep. And when I woke up Herman was downstairs on the phone and it was almost time for work. Just enough time to tell you about my ears, diary. And now that I've told you that I can probably tell you fucking anything. Because that's the weirdest thing I do. I think.

That and, also, maybe I mangle cats and leave them smeared across cold basement floors. That would be the weirdest IF IT'S TRUE. It's probably not true. I'm probably just bored.

Or maybe it's only true in patterned space. Which means it may as well not be true at all.

Either way, as soon as I get to the inn tonight I'm going to have to check the basement.

Tenth Entry

When I first got to work I considered telling Alf about my weird diary dream thing. Mainly because I didn't wanna have to go down and search the basement by myself.

But then I realized that the idea of telling Alf that I might have killed one of the cats, and running the risk of having him look at me like a crazy person, was a lot scarier than just going down into the basement by myself.

If I really killed one of the cats I definitely don't want Alf knowing about it. He would hate me. I would hate me. I like this relationship better when I know something terrible about him[29] and he doesn't know anything terrible about me.

---

29 Presumably she's referring to the fact that he watched and laughed while his sister drowned.

Scene of her
digging at her
head. Really
loud and wet
and fleshy
so the sound
overtakes the
image.

The spot on my scalp is so raw I can barely touch it. But it's also so full of new snags that I want to pick at, flaps I can pull up and dig deeper under. I started thinking about what my skull will look like when I eventually reach it. Will it be smooth? Or kind of abrasive like a cheese grater, all congested with flesh. How'll I get through it when the time comes?

Oh don't worry, diary, I'm JOKING. As if I'd crack open my skull, you fool.

I can't believe you're actually this worried that I'll crack my own skull open.

You must think I'm retarded.

Anyway, so, the basement is kind of crazy. I should explain it to you so you don't think I'm just being a pussy.

Nathanial Holcomb built it with the intention of making it a safe haven along the Underground Railroad, with big, thick, soundproof walls so no one can hear anything upstairs when the door is closed.

He was a doctor, too, and promised to give those slaves who ended up in his basement all the medicine and care they needed to heal up the scrapes and cuts and aches and pains accumulated on the journey so far. He used the big main area as sort of an examination room.

Along the wall farthest from the staircase are a bunch of little hallways that end in private rooms, where I guess different people and families could have some amount of privacy, or be able to hide in case any suspicious person came over.

That's just what Olivia told me, though. I've never seen any of the rooms myself. Because it's one of our rules to absolutely never ever go down any of the hallways. They're fucking scary. Completely dark, cobwebs draped across the thresholds, and sometimes we hear weird noises inside. Alf said once he'd heard a woman laughing.

And the cats hate the hallways, arch their backs and hiss and bounce away on the tips of their claws when they get too close.

Anyway, this was supposed to be a sort of ideal shelter for people in trouble, the kind of food, water, clean beds and special care they had never seen anywhere else. Nathanial made himself seem like someone they could trust. Which is a really nice idea. If it were true.

But according to town history, Nathanial Holcomb was a monster. He'd use the information he had about the people to make them do things. A lot of the kinds of things you'd expect, like he'd make them have sex with him and stuff. But also some things that I bet you wouldn't expect, like he'd make them fight each other. And he performed experiments on their bodies, like administering strange drugs that made people sick and documenting the effects. He performed unnecessary abortions on pregnant women and even amputated a man's leg.

My friend June's great-great-grandmother had been a maid here then. She told June's mother stories and June's mother told us, about how the help never knew what was going on in the basement, but the doors were always locked and bloody sheets always needed washing, and Holcomb himself was always covered in scratches and bruises, the kind a person might inflict before being quieted by a chloroform soaked rag. Once, June's great-great-grandmother found a picture sticking out from beneath a pile of papers in Holcomb's office, a diagram of two cadavers arranged in a way she'd never forget for as long as she lived. June pressed her mother for more details, but she just shook her head and began to burp, a prologue to vomit, and said, "I can't, June, it makes me sick. It makes me sick to even think about."

We get a lot of stories like this from June's

mother, [30] dramatic build-ups with very little pay-off. It drives June insane.

Anyway, Holcomb lived here till he died. Brain aneurism. Keeled over right there in the basement.

So, though Alfred and I talk tough about wanting to see a ghost, neither of us really loves being in the basement for long. Or all alone.

When you first go into the basement, you've gotta walk down this very tall staircase, with slats for steps, no risers in between, so anything could stroke or grab one of your unsuspecting ankles as you walk down the stairs. So you'd trip and fall and break your face or your neck and become just another permanent resident of The Boy Eats Girl Inn.

I always run up and down the steps as fast as I can so if there's anything hiding in the space behind them it won't have time to

---

30 It's hard to determine the validity of these accusations against Nathanial Holcomb. He was never convicted nor suspected of any crime while he was alive, and is in fact mentioned favorably in a number of historical texts about the Underground Railroad. However, many people in the town maintain this opinion, when you can manage to get them to talk about Nathanial Holcomb at all. Mention of his name to older locals, or even mention of the inn itself, elicits nervousness, discomfort, and in some cases aggression.

grab me. Another one of our stupid rules.[31] Probably if there are ghosts down there it wouldn't matter how fast I was running up and down the stairs. Or how many times Alf and I flicked on and off the lights before going down.

The great big main room, what was once Nathanial Holcomb's operating room, now has an industrial-sized washer and dryer as well as lots of cans. Paint cans. And cans of deck stain. And old brooms and mops and trays and rinsed margarine containers of bolts and other little shiny things. Hammers, mallets, screwdrivers. A shovel, a rake. A pickaxe.[32]

Great mur- ——— A pickaxe. What about that pickaxe?
der weapon! Something in me wanted to pick it up. Big
I see posters, and heavy in my hands, swoosh, swoosh
Halloween through the air so it nearly pulls my shoul-
costumes. The ders out of their sockets.
sequel is ten
years later, It made me shiver.
the inn now a There are lots of weird noises down there
popular wed- all time too, and not just stuff coming out
ding venue. of the hallways either, but stuff right in the
main room. A nail rolled off a shelf, the cat's
window suddenly slammed shut, the dryer

---

31 Rule 7: RUN up and down all staircases.

32 Presumably the murder weapon.

door groaning open out of nowhere. And these noises, these little disruptions to regular basement stillness, seem to increase in frequency the longer you're down there. More and more. Almost as though the sounds, the little irritations, are coming to something. Culminating. Threatening you to hurry up and get out.

So with the hallways being just too goddamn scary to venture into, and the sounds creeping me out every five seconds, this basement would be very difficult to search thoroughly.

The cat's window is newer, added when the inn was converted into an apartment building. It doesn't let in a lot of light, but enough so a person doesn't feel quite so totally enclosed down there.

I searched that big main room for a long time, behind the washer and dryer, in and around all the shelves, behind the big panes of glass that were meant a long time ago to be used for a sun porch that was never built.

The sounds were becoming more frequent than I'd ever heard before, warning me to get the fuck out. The sound of a creaking door closing shut oozed from the deep dark of one of the hallways.

I knew I really should check the hallways. I really, really should. Down one of those hallways is definitely where a dead cat would be. Break a rule and search the private rooms. Just the thought of it made me sick. They were so dark. So untrustworthy. No lights in there because we never used them. I'd need a flashlight. And to spontaneously grow an enormous pair of balls. Each dark-as-night open doorway seemed to be growling, daring me to come closer, you'll see what happens to you if you come closer. Large lolling tongues fixing to curl me into their basementy bowels.

And then I realized that not only had I not found a dead cat yet, I hadn't seen any cats at all the whole time I was down there.

Which was very weird.

Usually that open window had at least one cat peeking in from the outside, another one jumping through it, just missing Dean, asleep on the humming dryer, stirred awake by the sound of another cat landing next to him. Frank's yellow eyes staring from a high wooden shelf. Joey scratching at one of the thick wooden beams down here. The Rat Pack loved people. And just about any time they heard the basement door open, they all

rushed in or at least pried open sleepy eyelids, hoping to weave between feet, press up
against pant legs or get some food.

But there were no cats at all. None. And
the thought made cold hands wrap around
the base of my spine, work their way up
tight as though they were climbing a rope.

And suddenly the phone rang and I jolted
and ran up the stairs as fast as I could.

I just knew it would be my stupid fucking
dad. I knew it would be my stupid fucking
dad because it'd been a WHOLE HOUR
since the last time he called.

Eleventh Entry

I went to the front desk. Alfred was playing one single low note on the piano in the lobby.

DUN.

DUN.

DUN.

DUN.

"Boy Meets Girl Inn, this is Noelle."

"Hi sweetie." My father's small voice.

A lower note from Alfred.

DUNN.

DUNN.

DUNN.

DUNN.

"Hi Dad."

I waited for him to go next. I could always tell what the call would be about based on the length of time it took him to speak up. He was going to ask me a god-damn favor, that son of a bitch.

"Can I get you to pick up a roast chicken on your way home tomorrow morning?"

Okay, not so bad.

"Yeah, okay, I can do that."

"From Ollie's?" [33]

DUNNN.

DUNNN.

DUNNN.

"Dammit, Dad, that's way in the other direction!"

"I know, but I just got a flyer, they're on sale."

"I would pay the difference for that extra half hour of MY time. I bet the difference isn't even what I make in half an hour at this shit job."

Alfred noticed now that we were arguing.

---

[33] "Ollie's" is a local grocery store run by a man named Oliver Scrum. In his interview he claimed to know Noelle fairly well, saying that for years, at least four times a week, she was in there buying a roast chicken for her father. He said it had petered off as she got older and "likely began refusing," was how he put it. He said she complained about her father a lot. "I felt bad for the kid," he said. He'd had first-hand experience dealing with Noelle's father as well, as he'd often call and try to pressure Oliver into delivering a chicken.

He offered a sad sort of smile as he closed the piano lid and politely went upstairs.

"Please, Noelle, you know how I love the chicken from Ollie's."

I did know.

I have this memory of him eating his roast chicken from Ollie's. Greasy fingers slipping and sliding over goose-bumpy skin. Digging under and guiding those fingers between crisp dermis and flesh, easily rubbing away the unknowable sinews that had once held them together. Then pulling the skin right off. Stripping the little thing of its only protection. And eating it first. Pulling its bare flesh apart, slurping slivers of white and dark meat, sucking animatedly on each bone, rubbing grease against his teeth like a wired cokehead. His lips quivery, unable to predict where exactly his own fingers would be coming from in the torrent of his feeding.

I hate his lips so much. Too much saliva. Delicate, reluctant, and shaky. Like a pair of blind, just-born pink puppies. When they look as tiny and foreign and squishable as bugs.

"It will literally tack an extra half hour onto my walk. Do you have any idea what that's like when you're working a nightshift? You're asking me to enter into a fucking grocery store too. With all the people who have just woken up and the fluorescent lights. It's another wavelength, Dad. Please don't make me."

Of course you fucking don't know what it's like, you lazy bastard. I'm sorry I'm sorry. I know you can't.

"Please, Noelle. Could you just do this for me without a fight for once? I know, okay? I know I don't know what that's like but goddammit do you know what this is like? For me to be lying here, a crippled shithead, asking his daughter who has to more or less wipe his ass every morning and every night, to pick him up a goddamn roasted chicken? A seven-dollar pile of cheap meat and grease that's truly one of my only joys in life."

"Trust me, as the person who cleans the toilet, I know all about your love of grease. It's one of the other reasons I'm mad."

He laughed a bit. Because we had to laugh about things like that because otherwise it would just be too grim.

"Noelle, are you going to make me beg?"

"I should make you beg."

"Noelle."

"Fine, I'll get you the chicken from Ollie's."

You fucking nagging old worthless bitch.

"Thanks, honey."

"You're welcome."

"Have a nice night at work."

"Okay. Oh Dad, are you on hot water treatments [34] again?"

"Yeah."

"Okay, can you just try to make sure to leave me enough hot water for a shower?"

"Of course I'll try, Noelle. I always try."

"Yeah, alright. But you don't always succeed. I'm asking you to really TRY to SUCCEED on saving me hot water. Especially if I'll have just walked an extra half hour in the heat, to get you your goddamn roast chicken."

"Okay, yeah, I get it. See you, honey. I love you."

"Bye."

I slammed the phone down hard as Alf came back down the stairs.

"Everything okay?" he asked.

"Yeah, yeah, just the usual."

Alf knew all about the usual stuff. He knew how sick Herman was and I admitted to him that I found it so annoying I almost wished he'd just die. And Alf said he understood, said

---

34 A homeopathic treatment thought to restore energy to muscles when certain types of harmful blood bacteria are present.

that it must be hard for me, and he rubbed my back, which should have been nice but part of me wondered if he just liked the excuse to rub my back because he liked me, not because he actually cared about making me feel better.

I know, diary, I shouldn't be so negative. I know that Alf really cares about me, more than just my hole.

"I'll take the buzzer tonight," he said.

"You don't have to, Alf. It's my turn."

"No, I think you should get some sleep."

"Well, thanks," and I smiled at him.

Then we were quiet for a while. And he was looking at me, trying to form some kind of message to me with his eyes that I was pretending I didn't notice. But I could see it, quite plainly; see that he wanted to say something that would ruin everything. Looking at me in THAT WAY. It made me want to slap him across the face really hard, the way women do in old movies. Men seem to recover so quickly from that in old movies, like it was nothing, but I'm pretty sure if I flat-palm slapped Alf across the face he'd shriek and clutch his face and get very worked up. It would be a whole thing that we'd probably never stop talking about for as long as we lived.

And then he said my name:

"Noelle?"

"What is it, Alf." I tried to make it sound like a warning instead of a question. Like, don't you dare say it. And he must have noticed.

"Um, nothing." He coughed. "I, um, do you want to, did you ever get around to turning over the laundry? Or do you want me to do it?"

I didn't want Alf going into the basement. I didn't want him seeing anything down there I'd somehow missed.

"No, no, no, I'll do it, I'll do it."

"Okay," and he cleared his throat.

That wasn't what he was going to say but I didn't care. I'm glad he didn't say what he wanted to, because I don't wanna deal with it right now.

I went downstairs to flip the laundry.

No cats. No cats at all. Did I kill them all? Or have they run away? Because they're scared? Scared of what I did to Sammy, or what you say I did to Sammy? How can I trust you, diary, maybe you're lying. Maybe now that you're alive you wanna take over. Kill me and be the better me. Well it's not gonna happen, alright?

I don't know why I'm so mistrustful of

you. I guess because—I don't know. You'd betray me. You'd let anyone at all open you up and read about me. You're very disloyal, diary. I don't know why I put so much into something so very, very disloyal. And you make me look at myself in a way I hate. You make me see how crazy I am and you'd show anyone else too. Would you trust you if you were me? Jesus christ this is all fucking crazy too.

And, you know, things were fine before I started writing in you. I mean, they were miserable and hellish and depressing but otherwise totally fine.

Things weren't scary or insane or potentially dangerous at least.

But I also feel like, if I stop writing in you now, something bad is gonna happen. Like now that's I've started I can't stop. And I don't like that I can't stop now. I don't know.

Who are you?

Who ARE you?

WHO are you?

Who are YOU?

There's a fly down here. And it keeps landing on my head. Right on the sore spot. And it stings. And I remember reading once that when a fly lands it pukes and shits and then eats it but I'm sure that can't be true.

Probably just something someone made up to gross me out. [35]

But I don't like that it's buzzing around my head. Because flies buzz around dead things. Am I killing my head? Is it dead in that spot now? That one dead spot has passed on into some other dimension, another dimension in which Sammy is mostly dead and cold stiff fingers can touch me and I can hear and understand the whispering in the basement.

Dead Spot. Another potential title?

This spot on my scalp is pretty fucking zombie-bite gross.

Like ground meat left out, warm but not cooked. Hot soft. Hot soft. Hot soft. That's kind of making me nauseous the more that I write it.

Hot soft hot soft hot soft.

I need to stop picking.

Hot soft hot soft hot soft.

"Alf!" I called up from downstairs. "Do we have a flyswatter?"

---

35 While not technically true, flies often regurgitate digestive enzymes when they land on what they believe to be food. Flies defecate often, but not every time they land. That flies were possibly landing on Noelle's head is evidence of a potential infection; certain infections of the blood have been known to alter behavior. Blood samples, and samples of Noelle's flesh, are currently being analyzed.

"Yeah," he called down, "it's in the closet, kind of high up though. I'll grab it."

I heard him get up, his steps above causing dust to trickle from the ceiling. I swatted the fly away a few more times. Tried to kill it with my hand but missed. Then I ran up the stairs and slammed the door shut behind me, thinking maybe I could trap it down there. But it'd followed me up, buzzing around my head relentlessly so I had to keep swatting and spinning around.

Alf laughed.

"Maybe you should shower more," he said and handed over the lime green swatter.

"Maybe you should … shower more."

"Good comeback. I'll have to remember that one."

And Alf turned on the computer to play a game of Solitaire while I flailed around like a fool trying to kill the fly until it was time for us to go to bed.

I'm up in my room now, writing in you, and the fly has followed me up here too. The buzzing is so goddamn irritating, landing on my head, getting so close to my ear, making the sore spot itch so I scratch it and it bleeds everywhere. Stupid fucking fly. I wonder what my head meat looks like in his kaleidoscope eyes.

Maybe I should switch rooms.

But that's crazy. Switching rooms because of a fly. This has been my room all summer. It's right next to Alf's. He'd wonder why I want to move.

Olivia used to sleep in here. This was the room that Wink walked into, sat on her bed, and started eating her. Her NIGHTMARE.

I got a towel from the bathroom and wrapped my head up like a turban. There, nothing to attract the fly. And it seems to work. The fly disappeared. Or at least, it's stopped pestering me. But that was too easy. Way too easy. Maybe there was no fly at all. Maybe Alf thought he saw the fly too because I was spinning around and swatting like there was a fly there, but really there wasn't.

I took off the towel. The fly came back. So I put it back on.

Okay, time to go to bed. I'm glad I'm not sleeping with the buzzer tonight.

Thanks Alf. You're nice.

Twelfth Entry

Food water food water food water food water food water food water food water food water. Alive alive alive alive alive alive alive alive alive alive.

If Sammy dies then I die.

Because we're the same.

Food water for Sammy.

She watches from the corner and whispers and whispers and tells me that she's my friend and she loves me but if I kill Sammy then they've gotta do something bad. Something very very bad. Very very very very very very bad. She won't want to

What if Margaret is able —— to summon the son she gave up? He breaks out of some loony bin when she calls for him to come and kill off whoever she wants.

but she'll have to because Margaret opened her up and Margaret is her cruelest master.

And I'd deserve it. I'd deserve whatever Margaret does to me because little lives are precious apparently, even when that life is wheezing hacking suffering smeared and bored. Which is the worst of all. So so so bored. Always bored, always in pain, always sad. Because we're the same. My only joys are when he's sticking one in my ear and rubbing around and cleaning it out or I'm inducing a coma on a bedspread.

Sammy's hidden away downstairs. I'm hidden away too.

His fur feels so soft under my fingers, his little heart beating beating beating, fast as a bird. He's not losing a lot of blood. It's all stopped up and making his face swell and stink. His tongue is purple. His eye is all black now. But that little heart beats. That little miracle keeping this miracle alive. MIRACLE. Miracle. Miracle. Miracle.

Birth and death are always sure, each, in fact, as sure as the other. So how is birth a miracle? Miracles are supposed to be rare, extraordinary. Not something that happens every day.

And if birth is such a miracle, why is death a tragedy?

I said that out loud. I could tell I said it out

loud because she's shaking her head and saying SHHHHHHHH…

So I stop thinking about it and just stroke little Sammy till his beating heart slows a bit. He isn't scared because he's with me now. He isn't all alone anymore.

And she starts crawling towards me. I can see from the corner of my eye and I can feel her cold next to me and she puts her lips right up to my ear and asks me about the boy upstairs. Asks me if he deserves the patterned space we put Sammy in.

"Is he a good boy?" she whispers, and her voice feels injected into my ears, now lurching heavy through my veins like a disease.

"Yes," I say. "He's a very good boy."

"We wanna keep him?"

"Oh yes."

And she nods and whispers more and more and more and more and more. [36]

"Patterned space" is what makes Noelle special: the ability to travel to other ghostly dimensions. That's why she's the only one equipped to solve some Margaret-related mystery we'll come up with later.

---

36 This section is in the same wide scrawl as the last italicized section. Large and frantic and not quite like Noelle's regular handwriting. This section is nine pages long in the diary.

Thirteenth Entry

The next morning I woke up in bed. My bare feet were dark and dusty. Like the basement floor. I read and re-read what I wrote last night. Who is she, diary? You know her. You do. Margaret. She said that Margaret killed her. That Margaret "opened her up."

Alf stopped me as soon as I opened my bedroom door.

"Um, HI," he said, in a way like I was supposed to say something, or know exactly why he was saying UM HI like that.

"Um, hi," I said back, and moved past him to walk down the stairs.

"Aren't you going to say anything?" he asked.

"What?"

"Do you not remember anything from last night?" He seemed shocked.

"Alf, jesus christ, just tell me what you're talking about."

"Oh, I don't know, you scaring the ever-loving shit out of me?"

"What the hell are you talking about?"

"You set the buzzer off last night, you ass-hole, over and over again."

"No I didn't!"

"You did too! I came downstairs and you were laughing your head off, opening and closing the door. You know that's fucked up, Noelle. I'd never do that to you on buzzer night. And I did you a favor. Last night was supposed to be your night, but I took the buzzer for you."

"Are you serious?"

"You really don't remember."

"I really don't."

"I don't know if that makes me feel a lot better or a lot worse."

"What do you mean?"

"You were a goddamn maniac last night. Your eyes were really wide and kind of empty and creepy looking. And when I came down, you tore up the stairs and into your room and you were saying NO NO NO NO and you wouldn't open the door when

I was knocking. I thought you were fucking possessed."

"Yeah, oh my god, you know what? I was probably sleepwalking."

"What?"

"Mmhmm, yeah, it runs in the family. My dad sleepwalks. Or, he used to when he walked more. Now he just talks in his sleep a lot." That was a lie. Pretty obviously a lie. But Alf didn't seem to catch on.

"Well, maybe you should have told me that before. You know, being as we're working nights in a haunted goddamn inn."

"Haha, I'm sorry, Alf! Jeez, okay, now you know."

"Well, how often does this happen?"

"I don't know. It happens when it happens."

And he gave me a weird look. Kind of asking me with his face to tell him what the hell was wrong with me. But I didn't wanna tell him. Diary, I can tell you're judging me for not telling Alf the truth. I can tell. But I can't. I don't want him to think I'm crazy. I don't want him to know I hurt the cat. Alf thinks I'm great. I don't wanna ruin that. Even if I don't wanna date him, I don't want him to stop thinking I'm great.

I left him upstairs kind of flabbergasted I

guess. And I started walking in the opposite direction of home, towards Ollie's, where I bought Herman his goddamn chicken and had to make small talk with Ollie himself, who thought that because he supplied me with chickens, he could also supply me with unsolicited advice. Like that I shouldn't take a nightshift anywhere, especially not at the inn, because summers were for sunshine and fresh air, not for scaring yourself half to death.

Herman's face lit up when I dropped the chicken in his lap. Chicken at nine in the morning. I watched him eat it like a brutal bastard in the sickly white glow of the TV. His face illuminated as though by a snow-storm through a windowpane. He likes those courtroom shows the best. Judge Judy and The People's Court. He loves to weigh in on bitter family squabbles, petty theft, family members all feeling entitled to one sad reproduction painting that no one had ever really liked anyway.

Today I finally got up the courage to examine the spot on my scalp, close up in the mirror. It's gruesome. All dug out like my fingers were miniature excavators. It looks like a bit of pizza with the toppings pulled off. I wet a rag and daubed at it, but it was so sore. It made me wonder if there really was something to find under there. Something to excavate. Like how zits in commercials are apparently whole ecosystems when you finally get down under the skin.

Because it really was a bit softer, a bit tender, since that first time with poor Tucker. I couldn't resist squeezing at it a bit more even though it hurt. The pain felt good the way the sore spot could sometimes feel good. Savory pain, my favorite kind. A little blood burst spattered a line across the mirror. It startled me. I wiped it off.

Red and purple and blue salsa. My skull felt so close to the surface. I wondered if it would be sensitive to the cold, like teeth can be.

Then I knew I had to leave it alone for a while. So I went downstairs.

"Do you want any of this?" Herman asked without taking his eyes off the TV.

He was talking about the chicken.

"No thanks," I exhaled, plopping down into the chair next to his.

"Honestly, Noelle, this is the most delicious one yet."

"I'm glad."

"Really, they've never been this good before."

"That's because I poisoned it."

"You'd probably be better off, you know. You should poison the next one." And then he frowned at me for a minute before continuing.

"Can you believe this joker?" and he pointed to one of his courtroom shows on TV. "He's trying to sue this doctor here, this chiropractor, because his back didn't get fixed! I mean, come on, some people are just so entitled. That's what this is. I mean, chiropractors, they're not miracle workers. It's treatment, you know? That's what my doctor always says. It's a treatment, not a cure."

I nodded.

"Actually, honey, I made an appointment for you. Dr. Schiller says he hasn't seen you in two years. That's not good."

"When?"

"It's in a couple days. I put it in the calendar."

"Dad, I'm fine. I don't need to go to a doctor."

"Would you just please go? Look at me. It's not like you come from the best stock in the world."

"Fine."

"I wrote it in the calendar."

"You said that already."

And then I pulled my diary, you, out of my hoodie pocket. And wrote all this down just now while he kept on talking.

I don't understand why they had a kid at all. Why stupid Herman and stupid Roberta would ever do this to someone.

Roberta had been made mean early on, by an ugly skin disorder from age nine to seventeen. During that time, at some point, she'd met Herman. Funny Herman. Herman who could love anything with all his heart, really all of it, more than a regular person could be capable of, and he knew it, and it scared him. But in the hands of a spotted girl, skin as rough and angry as an orange peel, he felt safe. "No one would take her away from me," he thought. "She wouldn't even take herself away." So he let go and loved her hard, the way that only he could.

And she was very realistic about everything. She thought, "I don't want to be alone and no one else will ever love me, so I will be with Herman, funny Herman, and make him do whatever I want." Because don't forget, she'd been made mean.

And then one day she was cured. A miracle balm from Japan. So as soon as she could she cheated on poor Herman. Over and over and over again. Poor Herman, who thought he was safe and so had finally let loose, unloaded like explosive diarrhea his massive amounts of LOVE. It could never be recovered. He was broken. Unfixable. A water balloon burst.

He insisted she'd made him sick. Somehow in breaking him she'd caused his blood disease. She'd brought filth into the house. His colon spazzed. And she asked for a divorce.

He begged her for a child. To do that for him, for destroying him. And she gave in.

And had me.

I'm a parting gift, given out of guilt. The only reason I'm alive at all.

She knew. She knew on some level that leaving me with him would be torture. Torture that was rightfully supposed to be HERS.

I would be punished instead.

I existed because he wished for me.

It's not fair. Nathanial Holcomb should have cut me out of her, killed me then tortured her, locked her up in a little room for even *thinking* about forcing me to come to life.

I never should have been born, goddammit.

One day I'll show him. I'll show him

what a MISTAKE it was to have wished for me. To not have killed me when he had the chance, like a good person should have. Killed me. Or never wished for me in the first place.

Roberta.

I know that I have her eyes. Big and brown and set kind of far apart, but not too far. And I have her build: short but not fat. Long limbed and curvy at once. A good build. I'm glad I got it. I have her dark hair, too, and Herman says we have the same smile. I'm glad I never got her skin disease, what made her mean and spotted, what made her marry Herman.

It's a strange thought that you're probably as likely to have your mother's vagina as you are to have her eyes or any other genetic feature on her body. I wonder if I've got Roberta's.

And I wonder if it was her mother's vagina before it was hers before it was mine.

The only person who might actually know would be Herman.

Fourteenth Entry

Olivia noticed the cats almost right away, as I suspected she would. She came in from outside and then went down to the basement, which she rarely did. She said she was too crispy to risk a fall down the stairs.

But she was looking for the cats. She was worried about them, so worried it was worth the risk.

I kept quiet.

Alf and I were playing Crazy Eights in the lobby. Alf sitting with his legs crossed on the floor. I was lying on the piano bench, face down so I could see the cards, my dangling hair circling around our game like an arena, pressure growing on the sore spot when the blood rushed to my head.

Three days till the party. [37] Alf is going to get a bunch of beer soon and hide it in his room until Olivia leaves, then we'll stock the fridge, set out bags of chips and wait for everyone to get here. The whole thing is gonna take place in Margaret's suite. The very top floor. It's still a suite and could probably fit a hundred people, maybe even more.

It hasn't been occupied by a real guest in over a year.

"Alf? Noelle? Can you guys come here a minute?" Olivia sounded sad, worried. I could already see the look on her face from the way her voice sounded and it made me feel guilty.

We got up and met her in the hallway.

There it was. The face I'd pictured. Sad. Worried. Uneven eyebrows.

I don't know if you noticed, diary, but as soon as I saw that face of hers I started rubbing you in my hoodie pocket and just couldn't stop, ran my nail along your pages. It felt good to touch you like that when I was feeling so horrible with Olivia's trembling concern, her fear. And maybe all the answers, maybe all the terrible answers she'd never expect, were just inside my pocket, just inside you.

---

37 Therefore this entry was written on August 28th, 1999.

"Listen, do you guys know where the cats went?" she asked.

"The Rat Pack? They're gone?" Alfred answered innocently. Honestly.

"I have no idea where they went," I said. Because I really didn't have any idea where they'd went. But probably I should have pretended that I didn't know they were gone at all.

Olivia turned to me. "Noelle, you realized they were missing too? Why didn't you say anything?"

"Yeah, sorry. I just figured... well, I don't know what I figured. It's weird."

"It is. Very peculiar. I feel kind of worried."

"Oh don't, Olivia," Alf assured her. "They're cats, they do this kind of thing all the time. Once my cat disappeared, right? And he was gone for almost a month. When he came back he was all fat and sort of lazy. We thought he was going to die. Turns out he was a she and she was pregnant! Crazy, right? So then we had a bunch of cats. Eight. Oh, whoops, actually ten but she ate two. Anyway, we had to get rid of a lot of them and I guess we didn't let her wean properly because after that she ran away again, only that time she never came back."

Alfred was struggling. Olivia's eyebrows

were throwing him off. He wasn't ever going to stop talking unless somebody stopped him. So I did.

"Anyway, sorry I didn't say anything," I interrupted loudly.

Alf gave me a look of thanks.

"Well, thanks for that, Alfred," said Olivia politely. "I mean, I'm sure they'll come back. It just seems peculiar. Or like you said, Noelle, it's weird. They've never done this kind of thing before. When did you notice it?"

"Yesterday, I think."

And that made her look even more worried, that a whole day had already passed with them missing. So I pulled a hand from my hoodie pocket, from you, diary, and put it on her shoulder.

"I wouldn't worry about it," I said, and squeezed, and her body felt like a bundle of twigs beneath her shirt.

Actually, I probably would worry about it if I were her.

Because who knows, maybe I killed them all and buried them in the azaleas.

Did I, diary? Did I kill them all? You'd be the only one who really knows.

Her meter was almost all the way to the top so she said, "Okay then."

"Sorry, Olivia," I said.

"Yeah, sorry, I—" Alfred began, but I put my hand on his arm to stop him from launching into another idiotic monologue. He nodded at me.

"It's okay, guys. Look, I'm gonna get out of here. Make sure you take the garbage out before you hit the sack."

"We will."

"And call me if you find the cats. Don't worry about waking me up or anything, just call me, okay?"

"I promise we'll let you know," I said.

And she turned around and left out the back door, probably so she could take one last look around the yard. Poor Olivia. [38]

Alfred and I went back to our card game.

"That's weird," he said.

---

38 Olivia confirmed this conversation during our first interview. She said she'd noticed Noelle had seemed a bit off the past few days, but didn't connect it with the missing cats. "Why the hell would I?" she said, defensively. It's clear that Olivia feels a certain responsibility for what occurred here, likely because it was she who'd allowed the party in the first place. It was also she who'd been accountable for the nightshift for so many years before handing it over to "a couple of unlucky kids." A decision she'd expressed discomfort with from the beginning but felt was forced upon her both by her doctor, who insisted she couldn't work nightshifts anymore, and owner Anita Fray, who didn't have a lot of nightshift candidates to choose from.

"What?"

"That the cats are gone, obviously."

"Yeah, it's weird, but like, they're cats."

"No, I know, but they like it here. And all of them gone. Just weird, that's all. Why didn't you tell me when you noticed?"

"I don't know. I forgot, I guess."

And I couldn't help it but I raised a finger to the sore spot and started scratching hard. It'd dried a bit since last time so I worked up the scab, slowly separated its hardened perimeter from my squishy flesh, easier around the sides then tougher, more painful in the middle where the scab was deeper. Pulling there produced an eye-watering kind of pain, the sort of wincing that Alf might notice. But I got it off and rolled the scab up between my fingers quickly enough that he didn't notice.

But he did notice.

"What are you doing?" he asked, looking up at my head.

"Nothing," I said.

"No, what are you scratching at? Do you have lice, Noelle?"

"Fuck off, Alfred!"

"Geez, relax! That isn't the reaction of someone who doesn't have lice, you know."

"I don't have lice."

"If you say so. Do you wanna make a wish?"

"What do you mean?"

And then he reached towards me and pressed his first finger against my cheek and when he pulled it back there was an eyelash perched on the tip, as delicate as a butterfly.

"You've got a wish," he said. "You can wish to stop having lice."

I wished that Sammy wasn't lying smeared across the basement floor, but I didn't say that out loud, obviously. I closed my eyes and blew the eyelash into some other dimension.

"What did you wish for?" Alf asked.

"I can't tell you."

"I always wish for better-shaped eyelashes."

"What do you mean?"

"I have very annoying eyelashes. They're flat, not curved, you know? So when I get one in my eye it really hurts."

"Huh! I never realized that before."

"Does it look weird?"

"No, no, not on you, I just, I never realized that eyelashes are probably curved like that so they don't hurt your eyes if they fall in. They're kind of eye-shaped, sort of."

"Yeah."

"It's genius."

"Ha! Well, yeah!"

And for a minute I loved Alf for his weird straight eyelashes. And I loved that he consistently wished for the same thing over and over again. Like he believed on some level that there was a system; that if you spent enough time wishing for the same thing it might actually come true.

"Okay, you've gotta tell me yours now," he said.

"Quit asking me!"

"Come on, Noelle, I told you mine."

"Okay, I wished that the Manson murderers had cut Sharon Tate's baby out of her body after they killed her, and that baby was still alive somewhere, a baby boy, raised by hippie murderers instead of super rich Hollywood elite like he should have been, and that one day we meet and fall in love and get married."

Alf stared at me and then said, "What the hell is the matter with you?"

"I told you not to ask."

"That's not what you wished for."

"It is too."

"Well, I guess you did warn me." Alf was laughing and looking at me in an annoying way. I wanted to escape now. My head hurt. Probably that little baby boy was the only one lucky to die that night, because if he hadn't, those hippie murderers really would've taken him back to their weird ranch and turned him into a monster.

People shouldn't be able to turn other people into monsters like that. Kid brains should have some evolutionary safeguard against it. Because it's not fucking fair. Generation after generation of monsters; monsters who don't even know they're monsters. Like Herman. In fact, at this point in human history, I'd say no one in the world is un-monstrous enough to be responsible for molding another human brain. We should all just stop. Fucking Herman monster.

And then my Herman monster fucked-up brain hurt even more.

"Okay, I'm tired, Alf."

"What? You're going to bed?"

"Yeah, I'm still tired from last night."

"Come on, Noelle, it's so early!"

"I'm sorry, Alf, I'm just really beat."

"Fine." He sounded very disappointed. And maybe a little scared at the idea of being the only one awake and all alone. And it was his turn to have the buzzer in his room, too, so probably he didn't want to go to bed at all tonight. I should have offered to take it off his hands, like he did for me last night, but I really didn't want to.

And on any other night I would have stayed awake with him, I really would have. We stayed up all the time, most of the time even, but tonight my head was too sore. I needed patterned space too bad. I wanted to get back there, back to the basement, to see if Sammy was still alive, to whisper with whatever was down there, to find out what the fuck was going on in patterned space. Who knows, maybe my real eyelash wish came true and everything is actually totally fine in the basement.

But probably not.

Fifteenth Entry

She wakes me up. It isn't me. She wakes me up. Because she's staring at me and I can feel it so hard it wakes me up. It's funny how someone looking at you can be felt as distinctly as a touch or a grope or a bucket of water splashing over you. How does a body feel a stare? Where does a body feel a stare? Are those unflinching eyes touching me?

Fugue states will be shot from Noelle's point of view. We never actually see her, just the stuff that she's seeing.

I open my eyes right into hers, mine vertical, hers lying horizontally along the sheets. Big as robin's eggs and the same kind of wrong blue. As though they've been rolled in flour.

Peeking eyes. Not blinking.

Over the side of my bed.

I don't want to move or scream and startle whatever it is that makes her seem so likely to explode in a puff of flour. I don't want her to explode in a puff of flour. Her hands grip the side of the bed, nails broken to the slimy quick, the same flour stuck to them. Her lips floured too. All the spots on a person that are usually wet and sharp are floured and dull on her.

A long stretch of staring because I don't know what else to do. Then she stands up.

Long blonde hair and funny teeth that stick out as though they've formed around a gag.

"She could eat corn on the cob through Venetian blinds" my dad said about her once. I hear it in my head now. Margaret and Wink's famous last victim. I'd brought home a photocopied picture of her from the library. I liked the way she looked.

And Herman looked at the picture and said that about her.

About her.

About this floured woman standing in front of me.

This floured woman who died so many years ago.

She's famous because, according to Wink's diaries, this floured woman in front of me was the only victim that Margaret herself killed. And Wink said Margaret had tasted her blood and said it was like "sticky hot syrup," a quote the newspapers went crazy with. Sticky hot syrup. All over Margaret's fat face.

The floured woman's head seems too big for her long neck, which bends forward and bobs like a heavy flower. I can see what causes it to bob like that. And I remember too from the library's microfilm.

A long jagged scar across her neck, starting and ending in the warm thumbprints behind each earlobe. A bib of dark red, thick and wet. Sticky hot syrup. She moves her hand down, I think for a second to touch me, and my whole body clenches, blood suddenly ice, but she just grabs the glass on my nightstand and takes a drink and fresh wetness glugs from the slash in her throat, replenishing her bib, like she knows I'm looking at it.

She offers the glass to me, so I sit up and I take it and I pang my teeth against the rim. It should wake me up but it doesn't. So I'm either still sleeping or all the way awake. All the way awake in a place where I can see things like this floured woman. The last one to die. The last one to be killed by Wink and Margaret. But mostly Margaret.

I put the glass down and she reaches out her hand and I take her floury soft fingers and she leads me down the stairs. Quiet so we don't wake Alf. I hear her say shhhhhhhhhhhhhhhhh-hhhhhhhhh but I can't see her face because I'm behind her.

There are people in the lobby. Sitting in the chairs, sipping from white cups. Coffee. A doorman in a stiff uniform. Two pretty women behind the front desk. I hear a harp playing. A long-necked lady harpist pluck-pluck-plucking but I can't make out her face.

And a woman sits at the piano bench but she isn't playing. I can see her face better, but just barely. It looks like nylon pulled over a sharp skull. I can't see her eyes but I know she's staring at me. A man sits next to her. He's pulling up her skirt. The floured woman tells me not to look. That it's private. Then she leads me to the basement door, down the steps slowly so anything could grab my ankles but I don't think anything did and she says shhhhhhhhhh-hhhhh again but maybe not because I'm still behind her and can't see and she could be someone else now for all I know, the harpist maybe, or worse.

Then we're standing in the main room.

And again we're not alone. There are OTH-ERS down here. Faces scribbled out in spots but I can see enough to know which are lonely hearts girls and which were once hiding. Some walking around, some sitting on the dryer, on the floor. I see eyes in the shelves. Behind paint cans and gardening tools. I can hear footsteps upstairs, creaking ceiling, dust falling, real weight pressing down on the floors above. The OTHERS are everywhere. They're always everywhere.

And I've got a plastic bag in my hand. I open it and look inside at some wet cat food, a water bottle, and a flashlight.

Then the floured woman's blue eyes again are in mine. She's leading me down one of the dark hallways and then suddenly she's not. And I'm alone standing here, not even knowing which way to step. But I remember the flashlight and I take it out and cast a cone of light down the hallway and it moves as erratically as a pixie along the walls and everywhere and I think maybe this too should wake me up because I know at one point I laid the light across my own face trying to see what was going on in there, in my head. Wake up, Noelle, wake up and run away. Wake up wake up wake up. But I am awake and I feel good, comfortable, floating through the moistwarm cake of patterned space.

The OTHERS urge me in the right direction down the hall by making bad sounds in the wrong direction. Bad sounds like we're gonna lick you and bite you slowly and stick our claws into your soft little body. But still trying to be nice, to be my friends. Trust us. Whispering. TRUST US AND WE WON'T EAT YOU. And it's getting louder so I walk faster.

Then I hear groaning and I don't wanna go

towards the groaning either but it seems better than the bad sounds the OTHERS are making. So I keep going and I find a door and they want me to open it so I do and this is where the groaning is coming from. A sound that can't be from anywhere else. With all of the soundproofing and the thick walls of the hive-like basement where it seems OTHERS crawl about like bees all the time.

My frenzied cone of light falls on what groans. Here lies Sammy. In my spotlight. And I nearly expect him to leap up and start dancing like the Michigan Frog, top hat and all.

Sammy is in ecstasy. Floating through patterned space. His single, cloudy yellow eye staring up fishlike and stupid and happy.

Staring like the woman's floured eyes. Those must be the eyes of patterned space. Staring empty feeling good eyes.

The blood smeared around him is all black. Fur around the living eye all wet.

I put my flashlight down on the floor so its light falls against Sammy and our shadows are projected onto the wall.

On the wall we're massive.

On the wall I see the floured girl's shadow.

On the wall I'm not alone with Sammy.

But in the room I am. Alone. All alone.

My shadow reaches for him, pries open his

little mouth and scoops some of the cat food into it, press it into the back of his throat so his muscles consume it involuntarily, then sprinkle in water and stroke his exposed belly.

His paws, curled like dried potato bugs, twitch slightly. I touch one and it's so soft.

He groans again and I put my hand around his still-warm throat and think about killing him. I know I need to kill him. Suck him out of patterned space and into death's unknown calm. I know this is wrong. I know it. I look at the wall and see my enormous shadow with its hands around Sammy's neck and it looks right. So I say it out loud I think. Kill Sammy. Kill Sammy. But then I hear the whispering of those outside others. OTHERS. OTHERS telling me to let go of his throat. Trust us. Or else. Then her eyes are watching me. I'm looking into them somehow. They assure me patterned space is what he wants. My little friend deserves to be alive with them.

Because everything deserves the miracle.

The miracle of life.

I say, "But if I were him I'd want to die."

"Tsk tsk tsk tsk tsk tsk tsk tsk tsk tsk tsk tsk tsk tsk," a thousand tongues clucking at once, then they laugh at me, and I feel ashamed.

And I think again that I want to kill this little baby, little Sammy, but they're pulling my hands off of him, all inside with me now, whispering to me that a baby's life life life life life life is precious.

Margaret says it's so. Margaret says it's so. She saved her baby once. Lucky boy. He got to be the living, breathing son of murderers.

Seriously, ——— *FAMOUS!*
we need this
guy. We could   *But it doesn't sound that nice. To be the liv-*
have the best   *ing, breathing son of murderers.*
slasher fran-
chise of all   *It doesn't feel nice to be the living, breathing*
time on our   *daughter of Herman and Roberta.*
hands. We can
make it worth   *And I move my hands again to Sammy's*
his while. Tell *throat.*
him that.
                  And suddenly there is something in front of my flashlight. Something big and breathing heavy. Pudgy feet, red toenails, Margaret digs a fat finger TOO DEEP TOO DEEP TOO DEEP into my sore scalp and I scream and scream and scream. [39]

---

39 In Noelle's large, fugue-state scrawl, this section of the diary takes up twenty-six pages.

Sixteenth Entry

I woke up at the foot of the basement steps this morning. Obviously a terrible sign.

I almost went down the hall to check, to see if Sammy was lying there dead. I really almost did but then my stomach flipped so hard I couldn't move so I just ran up the stairs instead.

The day shifter was just settling in behind the front desk. This old lady named Jessica, [40] a friend of Olivia's. I think she might work here just for something to do. She sits at her desk and crochets all day and leaves all the shitty work for Alf and me. She'll list it out for us, too, out loud instead of just writing the jobs down, which is really annoying.

---

40 Jessica West, the woman who first discovered the bodies and called the police.

Examples:

"Somethin' got into the garbage back there, somethin' big. You're gonna wanna wear gloves. It's everywhere."

"The woman in Room 301, her dog just puked all over the rug, can one of yous help her out?"

"That homeless guy took a dump in the azaleas again, kids."

She took off her jacket and hung it next to the door and hadn't yet noticed that I was standing next to her.

"Jesus, Noelle!" She leapt when she finally noticed me. "You're gonna give an old lady a heart attack for crying out loud."

"Sorry, Jessica."

"Christ, what are you doing up already?"

"Couldn't sleep. I don't feel so well. I think I need to go home."

"Pardon my French, dear, but you look like dogshit."

"I'll also pardon the insult, Jessica, don't worry."

"Honey, I mean it. You should go to a doctor. There's blood on your head, for cristsakes. Why the hell is there blood on your head?"

I reached up and touched my face where blood had dripped from my sore spot. It was dry now, crusty, and flakes of it came off on my fingers.

"Oh god, yeah. I hit my head."

"I'm taking you to the hospital." She grabbed her purse and stood up. "Come on."

"No, no, Jessica, please. I'll go. Don't worry. In fact I've got an appointment tomorrow."

"Yeah, right. I'm calling your father."

"Jessica, come *on*, man! I'll go! Just trust me."

Then she looked at me for a while, and I didn't know what I'd do if she didn't just sit down and shut up about it.

"Fine," she finally said. "But if I find out you just went home and went to bed without talking to your dad or calling a doctor, there'll be trouble."

Jessica's nice. She really cares about Alf and me. But if she calls my dad I'll have to kill her.

"Okay, okay," I said. And I made my way towards the back door but ducked into the closet first. I needed a quiet place to write all this down, collect my thoughts before I have to go home and see Herman.

Jessica wouldn't come looking for me in here, and I could just leave quietly out the back door once she started nodding off at the desk over her crocheting. She literally wouldn't move the whole time she was here. She didn't drink tea or coffee or water because of her kidneys so she never even had to pee. She refused to tend to any guests beyond providing idle chit-chat while they waited for cabs in the lobby, or letting them know their needs would be met in a few hours when the nightshift crew came in.

I pulled the chain on the light bulb and it washed everything in the lantern's red glow and it sort of felt like patterned space so I could think properly without lying down.

I have to kill Sammy. I have to. It doesn't matter what they do to me. I can't let him live like that, all crushed and bleeding and hurt. If I let him live I'm no better than Herman, letting me live just so he doesn't have to be alone in hell.

And then suddenly the lantern over the bulb started spinning, slowly, so its dark red moved across the walls and my hands and your white pages.

Slowly slowly slowly. My heart beating so hard I could feel my ears projecting the sound like loudspeakers. My cheeks filled with piping hot blood, pumped too hard and fast. My fingers went stiff and I dropped my pen.

And the lantern kept moving, as though carefully controlled by a pair of hands as opposed to flicked once and allowed to ride its own momentum to a halt. To its death. And I imagined a pair of hands on me, moving me deliberately, stopping me, bringing me to a halt, to a bloody grinding end.

Hands leading me downstairs. Hands over my hands bashing Sammy's brains in. Hands over my hands grabbing that pickaxe and impaling my head on it. Hands over my hands making me open and close the door so Alf's buzzer would go off. Then I suddenly realized that maybe they wanted me to hurt Alf. I don't know why, but it felt that way. As though the hands made me buzz the buzzer to lure him downstairs. Would I have smashed his head with a paint can too? Kept him alive in patterned space?

Goddammit, diary, what the fuck is happening to me? Have I always been like this? Have I always done stuff like this in my sleep, in patterned space, but just never knew about it because I never had a diary to write it all down in?

And then the lantern stopped. Or the hands stopped moving it.

And after a long, frightening moment, the same deliberate slowness made the doorknob twitch, causing my eyes to spread so wide open they felt as though the corners might tear. I stared at the door and pushed myself back hard into the wall, almost toppling off the stool. The doorknob had been grabbed, held, and now it began to spin, so slowly. The taste of blood in my mouth. I'd been biting my lip.

It spun slow slow slow slow until I heard the click of the latch all the way tucked in.

I thought if the door starts opening, if it really does, then I'm going to faint, then it won't be my fault, I wouldn't have been able to fight or escape what was on the other side anyway so I wouldn't have to feel bad or mad at myself for it. I'd just faint and let whatever was going to happen, happen. If the floured girl wants to kill me or whatever, just, I'm okay with it. If Margaret is mad at me for trying to kill Sammy, okay I deserve it. I'll stay here forever as a ghost. And hey, maybe I'll kill Alf after all, so we can hang out forever. He wants that anyway, to work at the inn forever.

But nothing happened. The door didn't open. It just stayed like that, latch tucked all the way in, for what felt like forever.

So I just waited.

And waited.

And finally, in the exact second my eyelids began to relax, the chain on the light bulb ripped and I was in complete darkness.

I screamed at the top of my lungs and tore out of the closet, then through the inn's groaning back door, and I'm sure I fucking scared Jessica halfway to death.

Hopefully she didn't recognize my screaming. I barely recognized it.

I ran all the way home. Literally all the way. Like the little pig does. And when I got there I didn't want to go inside yet, so I sat on the front porch and I read and re-read and re-read those last weird pages of the diary. Again and again and again.

Something was in the closet with me, spinning my lantern.

And I knew, because I'd seen them all when I was asleep or not asleep and walking at night with the floured woman. People are everywhere at the inn. Ghosts. Are everywhere. Doing whatever they want. What do they want with me?

The woman's name, the floured woman, jesus christ it gave me a chill to write that. Her name is Sybil Groundwick. She was the last victim of Margaret Grimley and Wink. Her throat sliced open by Margaret; her blood "hot sticky syrup."

Wink. Wink died up in the suite too. Wink who probably did pull Olivia's flesh off in chunks and ATE IT. Wink whose last name no one knew. He said in his diaries that people would never ever find out his last name because the devil[41] had taught him to be invisible.

And no one ever did find it out.[42] No one would ever learn a thing about him except for what he left in his journals. So he got to be exactly who he wanted to be after he died to everyone. He got to write it all out just so.

Alf once said that people with no last names are superhuman. And they kind of are. Without a last name you get to just

---

41 Nathanial Holcomb's son, according to Wink's journals.

42 Confirmed. Though many searched extensively, no one was able to find anything else out about Wink except for what he'd left in his journals. Wink wrote that people would try to track him but that no one would ever break the old devil's spell that hid him. And to this day, that prediction remains true. His last name, his age, place of birth, etc. all remain unknown. Investigators couldn't even determine the prison at which he claimed to have shared a cell with Nathanial Holcomb's son. On the very slim chance that Hansel Holcomb was indeed serving time at more than 100 years of age, attempts were made by investigators to locate him. However, they discovered that shortly after the release of his father's essay on sensory deprivation and punishment, Hansel Holcomb changed his name and mostly disappeared, decades before he'd supposedly roomed with Wink in prison.

float through life, tethered to nothing and no one. I wish the devil had taught me to be invisible. I wish I was just Noelle. Instead of Noelle Dixon. The Dixon part tethering me to gross Herman and mean Roberta. Maybe if I didn't have a last name I wouldn't feel guilty either, about hating Herman or about maybe hurting Sammy.

I wish Nathanial Holcomb's son would put a spell on me too.

Teach me everything he knows about being invisible.

All of Wink and Margaret's victims were kind of lonely hearts ugly like Sybil.

Sybil was thirty-three when she died. She'd been corresponding with Wink and Margaret for a few weeks before she finally worked up the courage to come over. She'd said to her sister, "The only thing I've got to hold over the heads of married people is the opportunity to be wild." So she took it. Which, also according to her sister, was very unlike her.

I remember reading that quote. It made me like Sybil Groundwick very much. I liked people who rubbed things in other people's faces. No matter what they were rubbing in.

I liked her so I photocopied the picture of her from the newspaper. The best picture her family could find, I'm sure, so that people could think "she was so pretty, so young, she had her whole life ahead of her." And she wasn't pretty, but people don't ever say that dead girls aren't pretty. In fact, being dead is probably the best kind of makeover a girl can get.

That's probably why I'm dreaming about her. Because I liked her when I read about her, I really did.

But why am I fucking sleepwalking like a fucking psycho and then writing about it? Why can't I look down those halls, just see once and for all if I'm really doing the things I'm apparently writing about? Why is this happening now?

Noelle, you're not doing that. You know you're not. You love cats, that's crazy. You're just tired. You're not happy right now. Your dad is a lazy pathetic asshole who is ruining your life. That's all.

You're right, you're right. I didn't hurt any cats. I didn't. And you know what? If I did, it's not my fault. If I did it's because Herman Dixon let me be born. And he shouldn't have. Every bad thing I do is his fault, not mine. Because he should have known better than to wish me to life.

Monsters making monsters.

Herman was already wide awake and watching TV when I walked through the door.

He said, "Noelle! I just got off the phone with Jessica from the inn."

Goddamn you, Jessica.

"She says that you hit your head, sweetie, and that you don't look well. Come in here."

At least she didn't mention my screaming wildly out the door. [43]

He muted the TV. For him that demonstrated SERIOUS CONCERN.

"Hi," I said, stepping into the living room.

"Christ, Noelle, you look like a sheet!"

"I didn't get very much sleep last night."

"Let me look at your head."

"No."

"Noelle, I can see you're bleeding, now would you show me your head?"

"No!"

"Why?"

"It's nothing, I'm embarrassed."

"Well, if it's nothing, then show me."

"Okay, it's not NOTHING. I had a

---

43 In our interview, Jessica expressed deep regret that she didn't take Noelle to the doctor herself. She told us, "I never should have left it up to goddamn Herman to deal with."

giant zit on my head, I picked it, it leaked all down my face while I was sleeping. I told Jessica I hit my head because I was embarrassed about my weird giant zit."

"Why do you look so pale, then?"

"Because I didn't sleep!"

"Why didn't you sleep?"

"The rats in the basement. Those noises. I think they're crawling through the walls."

His face looked very WORRIED. I glanced at the television. He'd been watching one of those freak shows. Like, those shows that pretend to be uplifting, about people dealing with and sometimes overcoming a deformity or some kind of weird rare disease, but really the show is just for gawking. Like, you know, Siamese twins or really tiny people.

"Noelle. I want you to tell me if something's wrong."

"I'm fine."

"Honey, can you sit down at least? It hurts my neck to look up at you like this."

This freak show special was about a little girl born with her legs fused together. The narrator kept calling her a mermaid. [44] I sat

---

44 Sirenomelia, or Mermaid Syndrome, is an extremely rare congenital deformity in which the legs of an infant are fused together.

down and he started talking. While he talked I pushed my legs together and imagined they were fused.

"Look, Noelle, I know why you wouldn't wanna tell me. You don't wanna add to my stress. I get it. It's sweet. But listen, honey, it's not your job to protect your daddy. It's your daddy's job to protect you. I'm here for you, okay? I know it doesn't always seem that way. I know I haven't been a great dad. I know that. But goddammit I've done my best. You don't know what it's been like for me, sick the way that I am, having to watch you do everything for your old dad, walking to Ollie's all the time to get my chicken, helping me keep clean. I love you so much, Noelle. You know that. I love you so much it hurts. And I've had to watch as I ruin your life. Do you know how that feels? I'm ruining your life and I can't stop!"

And his voice shook so hard. He wanted so badly to seem so sad and pathetic that I would have to love him.

And jesus christ can't he say ANYTHING else at all, EVER? Is this really all he has to say to me right now? That he's pathetic and sad and guilty about ruining MY life? I'm pale and bleeding and pretty obviously NOT OKAY.

"Yeah, I get it," I said. "I get it, Dad. But just, really, there's nothing wrong with me. I feel fine. Don't listen to Jessica. She's just a bored old woman with nothing better to do than fret about people who don't even like her."

"I like Jessica."

"You would," and we both kind of laughed. I like Jessica too.

I went into the kitchen and got a glass of water. The mermaid show was over. Now a show about a boy born without a face was starting. We'd watched this one before. The boy had just a mash-up of sore-looking folds and three holes in his head where a face should be. He ate through a feeding tube. He couldn't speak or see or taste anything. He was at risk of dying from a thousand infections a day. But his brain was fine. He realized how disgusting he would be forever. But he was a miracle too, according to his parents; monsters who didn't know they were monsters. We're all miracles. A beating heart is a miracle no matter what kind of flesh it animates, no matter what kind of life that animated flesh is living, no matter if it's ground into a basement floor or slave to a terrible Herman. I felt like puking. To stop the puke I chugged back the glass of water. And then another one.

Herman yelled from the living room: "Dr. Schiller called to confirm your appointment. You better tell him about your zit."

"What time is that appointment anyway?"

"4:45. Before you go to work."

"Ugh, Dad. I don't want to go."

"Noelle, would you please just do this for me?"

And I stomped up the stairs. Loud so that Herman knew I was mad and every stomp was like a stomp on his face.

Just do this for me. Just do this for me. THIS ONE LITTLE THING FOR ME. THIS IS ALL I ASK OF YOU, NOELLE, JUST TAKE CARE OF YOURSELF FOR YOUR OLD DAD WHO TAKES CARE OF YOU.

I'm fucking exhausted and confused and I needed to feel what was going on in that spot because it felt bad. Really bad. And there was really an awful lot of blood on my face. And my hair was all dried too stiff and straight. And I suppose I should feel thankful that they care, Jessica and Herman, but I know they'll just tell me to stop digging at my head. Stop digging. And I can't stop.

How bad does it look, diary?

Ha, that was weird. I just held you up to look at my head even though you don't have any eyes. Jesus, I'm tired. I'm tired and hating Herman makes me even more tired.

What an asshole. Somehow he just managed to get mad at me for being mad at him for ruining my life.

He's broken me. He's broken me because he couldn't break her for breaking him.

This is too confusing. It should never be this confusing. Kill a person before their life ever has to be this twisted up.

And I fell asleep for the whole day at home because I didn't want to fall asleep at the inn, because when I fell asleep at the inn these days weird things showed up in my diary and I didn't want that to happen anymore.

Herman was asleep in his chair when I left later, and I imagined wrapping his housecoat belt around his neck and squeezing tight so all the veins in his neck filled up and his face went purple and spit flew from his mouth when he said please no please please Noelle no, and his eyes bulged till they turned red and popped and splattered in my smiling face. I would do that to Herman. But I wouldn't do it to Sammy, not Sammy who'd never done anything bad to me except weave around my feet, slowing me down when I tried to RUN up or down the basement steps.

When I got to work, Alf was already there. "Where were you this morning?" he asked.

Usually we saw each other before we left for home, walked a very short part of the way together before splitting at a corner that separated his nicer part of town from my shittier part.

"I couldn't sleep, so I just left when I heard Jessica."

"Oh."

"Sorry."

"It's okay. Just didn't know what happened to you."

"I'll make it up to you. I can take the buzzer tonight."

"You don't have to do that."

"No, it's okay. I want to."

"You want the buzzer?"

"Yeah, why not."

"Listen, Noelle, are—"

And he was definitely going to ask me if I was okay, he was going to tell me I looked awful, he was going to be CONCERNED, and that was going to make me very angry and maybe say something I'd regret, so I cut him off.

"Do you want to play cards?"

"Well, I was going to—"

"Please let's play cards. I'll actually die if we don't play cards right this second."

And he gave me a weird look but he grabbed the cards anyway, and I made a giant pot of coffee. And when Alf got tired and wanted to go to bed, I grabbed the buzzer and took it to my room. And I lay on the bed and I stared at it, hard, thinking about Dr. Schiller peeling back a sheet of my matted hair, seeing my scalp, gagging, calling in a colleague, saying you've gotta take a look at this, then both of them peering into my head, seeing patterned space, sticking their fingers in there the way she had, their fingers warmer, not right, not cold like hers. Patterned space that I wanted so badly but definitely couldn't drift into right now, not now, or maybe I could. Maybe I should drift into patterned space and kill Sammy like I should have last night. Who cares what they do to me because I don't want to be alive anyway.

And all night the house was the conspicuous quiet it is when we have guests. Except we didn't have any guests. It was being conspicuously quiet because it knew I was awake. On guard and watching it. And it would never show itself this way. Because it could be kind of a dick like that.

Seventeenth Entry

So all night, nothing happened, and even though I should have been happy that nothing happened, it made me feel even more nervous. When I got home I was exhausted and slept all day. Then I ate a bowl of cereal with Herman in front of the TV for dinner before I left for my doctor appointment. He told me he was feeling better than he had in years.

"Yeah, my energy's up. I think I might even go on a walk tonight."

"A walk."

"Yeah, I might go down to Ollie's and pick up a chicken."

"You're going to walk to Ollie's yourself? Jesus, I feel like we need to celebrate or something."

"Oh stop."

"No really, I'm going to call ahead and have them get balloons and make it so, like, confetti shoots from the register when you check out."

"Look, if you'd rather I didn't walk there myself, then you can just grab another chicken for me after work."

"No, no. I'll believe it when I see it, that's all."

"Listen, Noelle, for your information, I think it's that last chicken you bought me, as a matter of fact. I think it's turned me around. I've been feeling better and better since I ate it."

"Quick, someone alert the press, local greasy chicken establishment cures blood diseases, irritable bowels, and chronic uselessness."

"Well, someone's bitchy today. I should call and warn Alf."

"He's used to it."

"Well, joke if you want to, but I really have been feeling great since that last chicken, and I won't let you ruin it for me."

Ruin it for you. HA! I brought you the goddamn chicken. The cure-all chicken. You fucking idiot. I brought you the cure-all chicken, I saved you, you ungrateful fuck.

He just wants me to remember how I moaned about it. He wants me to think, "And can you believe it, Noelle? That you almost didn't get him that chicken? Can you believe that you almost KEPT your father from feeling good and healthy? What's the matter with you?"

You rotten little stinking ingrate. You fucked-up little person who can't even love her mother and her father when they're both wrapped into one feeble blood-diseased body. You wished you could strangle him with his housecoat belt, you wrote it here yourself, his blasted open eyeball blood all over your face you little fucking asshole.

No, that's not true. I don't want that. I want him to be better. I do. My life will be better if he's better. But god dammit, you're right, I also want him to suffer, not to die, but to suffer. I want him to be suffering when I leave him forever.

No I don't. Diary, I don't. Forget I said that. It's hard now that you're alive. I can't just scribble things out and expect you not to remember.

I'm probably going to have to kill you at some point. Throw you into a fire so no one ever sees any of this.

Eighteenth Entry

All the usual stuff at the doctor's office. Height weight ears blood. Blah blah blah. Every time I'm at the doctor's office I expect to hear that I've contracted my father's blood disease or his irritable bowels. A picture swirls into my head, the both of us totally weak, incapable of taking care of ourselves, dying alone in the house, bodies rotting in our respective TV chairs. It would be so long before anyone noticed, the stench of our irritable bowels excreting as slowly, heavily, as the life leaving our bodies.

Instead, this time all I got was a short lecture from Dr. Schiller about how important annual check-ups are and how I'm going to start going around my dad and scheduling them myself.

"He's got a lot on his plate, dear," said Dr. Schiller. "How about you just start scheduling them with Rita yourself?"

"Okay."

He checked my reflexes, which were fine. He asked me to keep an eye on an irregularly shaped freckle on my shoulder. I thought of a movie I saw once about a devil in a human body, a strange mark on his shoulder the only hint of his true form. Maybe I'm a devil. Maybe that's why I'm able to see the inn's ghostly stains. Only a devil would hurt sweet Sammy the way I had or hate sick Herman the way I do.

"Anything you wanna talk about?" he asked.

"I don't think so."

"You're not experiencing any pain or anything anywhere?"

"Nope."

"Everything's okay at home?"

"The usual."

Diary, shut up, shut up. Would you shut the fuck up? I wasn't about to tell him about my head so just stop it. If you don't stop it I won't tell you anything ever again.

"You're looking a little pale," he continued. "I'm going to give you a form for blood work and have them check your iron. You promise you'll go?"

"I promise."

"Okay. Noelle, do you mind if we talk about your father for a minute?"

This was weird. We've been seeing Dr. Schiller for years and years and never once has he ever brought Herman up with me. Not like this, anyway.

"Okay."

"Now, normally I wouldn't do this. But Noelle, I know you're a mature young lady, and frankly I just don't know who else to talk to about this. I've tried to discuss it with Herman, but you know how he is."

I do know how he is, so I nodded.

"Noelle, I'm starting to think that your father's health issues are, well, that they're psychosomatic."

"What does that mean?"

"Well, it means that there might not be anything actually physically wrong with him. That all of his health problems are in his head."

"What?" I whispered. And I could feel my face turning bright red. Nothing wrong with him. NOTHING WRONG WITH HIM. NOTHING WRONG WITH HIM.

I think Dr. Schiller noticed that my face was looking angry instead of concerned.

"That doesn't mean he's not experiencing these health issues in a very real way, Noelle," he said sort of sternly. "It's just that there really doesn't seem to be anything wrong with his blood, or his colon, or anything else he complains about."

"Okay, so what do we do then?"

"I want to recommend a psychiatrist."

"So recommend one. God knows he'll be in here again soon."

"Well, like I said, you know how your father is. The mere mention that his symptoms might be psychological made him so defensive."

"You told him this already?"

"Yes, the last time I saw him."

"Last week?"

"Last week? Noelle, I haven't seen him in over a year." [45]

"What?"

"I haven't seen him since, oh, summer of last year I think."

"But he said, he told me he's been coming in all the time like usual."

---

45 According to Dr. Schiller's books, Herman hadn't been in to see him in fourteen months. We cross-referenced this with the Dixons' kitchen calendar, which showed what must have been false appointments scheduled twice a month.

"Well, um, I don't know what to say, Noelle. He hasn't been. I haven't seen your father basically since I suggested to him that his condition might be mental as opposed to physical."

Liar fucking liar pig face liar.

"I'll talk to him," I said. And slid off the crunchy papered bed.

"Now honey, please tell me if this is awkward for you. I don't want to put you in this situation, but you understand I don't know who else to talk to about this. And I know you want him well just as much as I do."

"I said I'll talk to him." Oh, I'll talk to him alright. I want to fucking talk to him. I want to fucking kill him for making me take care of him for all these years when nothing is the goddamn matter with him. FOR LYING TO ME about even SEEING Dr. FUCKING Schiller. LYING. All the time, lying.

"Thanks, Noelle. Okay, talk to Rita. I want to look at that freckle again in six months. And you promised you'd get that blood work done."

"I know, I will."

And I took a sucker before I left. And I opened it up and bit it and crunched down angry on the hard sugar.

It felt good.

A sharp section of it cut my cheek a little and that kind of felt good too.

And of course I dug my finger into my scalp. And that felt really, really, really good.

And now I'm on the bus on the way to work, writing, writing away, and I want to squeeze Herman's throat shut with my bare fucking hands. Fuck the housecoat belt, I want to feel his skin between my fingers, his pulse pounding, pounding, then gone, just like that, and all because of me.

Psychosomatic. Psycho-goddamn-somatic. Meaning he's just a goddamn lying fuckface.

Meaning there's nothing wrong with his colon or the goddamn muscles in his sphincter.

Sick bastard, ruining my life for no good reason.

I'm not the one who should have been aborted. He is.

I'll show him. I'll show that lying son of a bitch monster.

Nineteenth Entry

Needless to say, I'm feeling very distracted at work. Alf is drawing a picture of the lobby in pencil; he's decided to try his very best to see if he doesn't have some latent artistic skills.

I'm glad he's preoccupied. I don't wanna talk to anyone but you, diary. I don't know what to think so I'm just going to write.

The phone is ringing. I know it's going to be Herman. I know it. The ring is so much more annoying when it's Herman. And shit. I'm closest. If I ask Alf to get it he'll wanna know why I can't answer it myself. He'll definitely ask me what's wrong. Fuck it.

It was Herman.

"Hi, honey."

"Hi, Herman."

"How was Dr. Schiller?"

"He was fine."

"Oh, sweetie … "

"What is it?"

"Trying to walk to Ollie's was a mistake."

"What happened?"

"Well, I started walking and I was feeling great. I really was. Maybe not 100 percent, but better than I've felt in years. And you know what? I think that, I think that I was just so happy to be feeling even a little bit better at all that I really overestimated my abilities. I should have just stuck to what I was doing: resting, drinking lots of water, our treatments, you know. Anyway I was walking to Ollie's and suddenly I felt very faint. There were big spots in my vision that were all blurry and my heart was beating so fast. Oh, Noelle, it was terrifying."

"I'll bet."

"Anyway I thought I was going to faint. I really did. So I sat down on the curb and this very nice woman came up to me and asked me if I was alright. She said she'd seen me from her window and was worried about me. I must have looked really bad. She asked me if I needed her to call an ambulance. I said, oh, you know, you're so sweet. Do you think you could call me a cab? So she did. I hope you don't mind, Noelle, I used some of the cash in your room to pay him. I didn't have any on me."

"Right."

"You don't sound very concerned."

"Well, obviously you're not dead. What do you want me to do?"

"A little concern would make me feel good, I don't mind saying."

"No, you don't mind saying. That's part of your problem."

And then he took one of his long pauses. These long pauses in which I was supposed to think he was holding back tears, so I was supposed to just start apologizing. But I didn't. I didn't say anything.

The length of this pause was infuriating.

"Well, Noelle, what I'm trying to say is, I'm not better. In fact, I'm feeling worse than ever. I need you to come home, honey, and help me."

"I can't. I'm working."

"Noelle, please. I almost fainted today. I need you."

"Herman, I'm not coming home. If you start to die, call an ambulance."

And I slammed the phone down. Alf was staring at me.

"What?" I said.

"Was that your dad?"

"No, it was a telemarketer."

Alf laughed and returned to his pencil drawing. And I wrote all of this down in you.

Diary, what am I going to do? What am I going to do? What am I going to do? What can I do? Hearing his voice makes me wanna ram pencils into his eyes. I won't be able to look at him. I hate that lying creep so much it's eating up my brain worse than ever.

Twentieth Entry

At 3:00 a.m. tonight a sudden crashing noise upstairs, the suite, Margaret and Wink's apartment.

Alf and I both threw open our doors at the same time and then startled each other and screamed and then laughed our heads off and then looked up at the ceiling, the suite just above us. Where the crashing sound came from. I thought I might have heard footsteps but Alf said he didn't. And even though the crash scared me half to death, I was relieved the house had made a sound, relieved that it wasn't just being watchful and quiet like last night.

We decided to head downstairs, to the kitchen for a midnight snack and to maybe play some cards or walk through the hallways

Black screen when we hear the crash. Then Noelle hits the lights and her weird-sexy/terrified face fills the shot.

with a knife or an umbrella or some other makeshift weapon, half-heartedly looking for ghosts but not really looking for ghosts, because of the RULE. [46]

When these things happened, big "bumps in the night," we were never able to sleep after. And in a weird way I think we both kind of looked forward to them. These nights make up the stories we'll eventually tell about our days working at the haunted inn. If Alf and I can be friends forever then we could even tell them together and reminisce about how fun it was to sit up all night long and drink coffee after coffee. We'd do the annoying thing that people who have known each other forever do, interrupt with details while the other one has the reins of the story, talk at the same time, laugh together over the bits that really aren't that funny if you weren't there.

Naturally Alf flicked the kitchen light five times before leaving it on.

We both looked around from the open kitchen door. The coast appeared to be clear. But of course I knew that if we were in patterned space this kitchen would be crawling with mumbling OTHERS.

---

46 Rule 2: Tell yourself you want to see a ghost if you really DON'T want to see a ghost.

"Make coffee, Alfred," I demanded.

"You make the coffee."

"Ha, please. Go make coffee."

"Why?"

"Because your name is Alfred! Blame your parents, not me."

"Can you come in with me?"

"Oh, fine."

So I followed him into the kitchen and watched him work.

"Party's almost here," he said, pulling the big coffee can from above the sink. It's tomorrow night. Or, technically, tonight.

"Yep."

"I hope something crazy happens."

"Like what?"

"Well, I don't know. You know what I mean."

"Like something spoooooooooooky?"

I grabbed our respective mugs, mine brown with sort of puffed-up pumpkins on it and Alf's white and plain with some law school crest embossed into the side. We always use the same mugs for some reason.

Olivia only drinks tea and she does it from a real teacup with a tiny handle hardly big enough for her finger's wrinkled tip. Real teacups are too small. No room for sloshing around so they're impossible to carry anywhere. Those cups force you to sit and be seated and do nothing but sip. Maybe that's why ladies in Victorian movies are never DOING anything. Bound to the table by their teacups. Bound to the table by THE THREAT OF MESS.

"Yes, obviously something spooky. Do you know how cool that would be? Not only are we throwing an Anniversary party IN Margaret and Wink's suite, but if something actually happened too? It would become a legend."

"When are you getting beer?" I asked.

Alf held up a hand to show that he was counting scoops and couldn't be distracted. I gave him a look like, you really can't talk and count to twelve at the same time? And he gave me a look back, like a retard-face look.

"Tomorrow afternoon," he finally answered.

"Are you gonna use your ID? Or are you gonna get Dwayne to do it?" Dwayne is an older kid. Kind of a weirdo who is always up for buying younger kids beer in exchange for an invite to a party. He likes to mac on younger girls and always tries to impress everybody with how much he can drink so usually he ends up sprawled on a lawn some-where, a crumpled island in a sea of his own puke by midnight.

"I'll do it. I don't wanna deal with Dwayne."

"You better not fuck up, Alf."

"Um, yeah, I know, Noelle, but thanks for the hot tip."

"I better not be beerless. Otherwise I'm going to make you break into your dad's liquor cabinet. And you know how you hate that."

"I hate you."

And I shoved his coffee mug at him fast, across the table so it slid too close to the edge. I don't know why I did that. It was kind of stupid. I didn't want Alf's mug to break.

"Whoa! Watch it, psycho! I'm just kidding."

"I know."

And then Alf gave me another weird look, but this one was sort of scared, like, "Okay, dear god, please let me ask you if you're okay" without actually having to make things weird by saying out loud, "Okay, dear god, please let me ask you if you're okay," all serious and annoying.

"Okay, we're awake now." I decided to change the subject. "What should we do?"

"Well, I was thinking maybe we could take the Ouija board up to the suite. See if we can't get things going in there. We won't have time before the party."

"Are you fucking retarded, Alf?"

"What do you mean?"

"Why would we go up there in the middle of the goddamn night with a Ouija board? Does anyone REALLY do that? Except for people in movies that are about to be brutally murdered?"

"Wow, you're really scared. Okay fine, we don't have to."

"I know you're scared too. Why would you flick the lights five times if you weren't scared of something?!"

"Of course I'm scared, Noelle, that's why I wanna go up!"

"To just, feel horribly scared?"

"Yeah, obviously."

"But what if something happens?"

"If something happens, that's even better."

"I don't know, Alf. If this were a movie, I'd be yelling at us not to do this."

He was quiet for a minute before he spoke again, contemplating whether or not to say what he wanted to say next.

"Okay, I'm just going to ask. Are you okay?"

I must have sounded too serious about not wanting to go up.

"Yeah, of course I'm okay."

And that probably sounded too defensive.

"Noelle, no you're not. You love getting scared. We've talked about this. We heard a crash in the suite. Tomorrow is the Anniversary. Are you seriously considering NOT taking a Ouija board up there?"

"Okay, fine, let's go upstairs."

"Look, I'm sorry. I don't mean to be a bully. We don't have to."

"Alf, don't flatter yourself, you couldn't be a bully if you tried. I want to go up. You're right, it'll be fun."

Because maybe it's Sybil up there. [47] And maybe we can see her for real this time. Not just in patterned space. Maybe Alf will see her too and maybe I can tell him everything and then it'll all be okay.

"There you go. It will be fun. I know sometimes this place can be weird, it can kind of get to you, right?"

I nodded because I couldn't get the word YES out. My throat suddenly felt all pulled tight like the strings on a hoodie closing up. And I wondered then, for the first time, if

---

47 Preliminary conversations with child psychologists hired to work on the diary reveal that this line holds particular psychological significance: the point in which Noelle seems to want to conflate her real world with the unreal world of "patterned space."

maybe Alf was having his own strange experiences as well, maybe it was something HE did to make the cats disappear. I fucking hope so. I really would rather the missing cats be all Alf's fault somehow than mine.

"So I get that maybe you're just having a weird night. I don't think you're chicken. Okay? We don't have to go upstairs."

And I smiled. And poured us big cups of coffee, then destroyed them with cream and sugar. That's what Herman says when I fix coffee. That I destroy mine. He likes it black because it kickstarts his spastic bowels.

"Alfred. I'm fine. But thanks for caring. It's sweet."

And he turned so red, especially his ears, and I got up and left the kitchen before he could shift into anything I didn't want to talk about.

We kept the Ouija board in the closet near the back door. On the very top shelf, near the back so we had to grab for it up there without really being able to see. I tried but couldn't find it with my splayed, reaching fingers. And then suddenly I felt very scared to be reaching into darkness like that.

I went back into the kitchen and grabbed a chair. Alf was just getting up to refill our coffees. I pulled the chair to the closet and peered over the shelf.

The Ouija board was gone.

I got down from the chair and walked down the hall to the lobby.

The Ouija board was sitting on the front desk.

"Oh you got it already?" asked Alf, our topped-up coffees in his hands.

And for some reason I said, "Yes, I got it."

I don't know why I said yes. I should have said, "Um, no, I didn't, Alf. It's pretty fucked up, though, that something in this house seems to want us to go up to the suite and use it though, right? In fact, maybe we should just forget it and go back to bed."

But I didn't say that.

Instead of saying that, I grabbed it and ran[48] up to Margaret and Wink's top floor suite.

---

48 Rule 7: RUN up and down all staircases.

Twenty-First Entry

The suite had changed a lot since it was Margaret and Wink's apartment. After it became a hotel, management hired a man named Claude to totally redecorate the inside, probably so that it looked absolutely nothing like the way it had in the pictures all over the newspaper, filthy and spattered with blood and grease and vomit.

The last two fingers of each of Claude's hands were fused together, one mega nail and a wide joint. Olivia had met him once a long time ago and told us she didn't notice his fingers till she was already shaking his hand.

Claude had employed a then-modern, now very dated-looking Southwestern motif, those sharp, almost offensive Mexican prints, a mess of decorative arrows and turquoise stones, strips of leather on the floor and cow-hide pillows that were prickly and uncom-fortable.

Alf and I sat in the middle of the room, Alf with a cowhide pillow over his crossed legs, his arms lying overtop to reach the planchette. [49] I made a cushion of my calves and the convenient curve of my socked heels. The way my father begged me not to sit because I'll "ruin my knees!" Hot coffees steamed next to us on the floor.

"Alf, what's with the pillow?"

"What do you mean?"

"Are you planning on getting a boner tonight?"

"What? No!"

"Then what's with that boner-hider pil-low in your lap? Get rid of it, it's weirding me out."

"I can sit how I want!"

"Please, Alf, you look like a fat girl, come on."

"What do you mean?"

"It's a classic fat girl move, sitting with a pillow on your lap. I do it all the time."

"You're not a fat girl."

---

49 A small, heart-shaped piece of wood used to move around the Ouija board and indicate or spell out the message on the board.

"Okay, well, neither are you so lose the pillow, okay?"

"Noelle, you're so edgy lately."

"I'm always edgy."

"Okay, fine, but lately it's been worse. You know what I'm talking about. What the hell is the matter with you?"

Let's see, why am I on edge? Could it be the fact that Alf has this frustrating goddamn crush on me? So that we can never be friends forever now? Or what about the fact that I'm walking in my sleep and seemingly interacting with ghosts, or that I'm abusing Olivia's poor cats? Could that be why I'm edgy? OR WHAT ABOUT THE FACT THAT MY FUCKING FATHER IS A FUCKING LIAR!

I took a big gulp of my coffee, hoping it would distract me. "Nothing is the matter, okay? Now let's do this. Who do you want to contact?"

"I don't know. Probably Wink or Margaret," Alf suggested.

"What about the big guy?" I asked.

"Nathanial Holcomb?"

I nodded.

"I think he's in the basement."

"You don't think they're all just everywhere?"

"I don't know if it works like that."

I happened to know that it did work like that. Because I'd seen it.

"I guess either way, this is Margaret and Wink's apartment so they're probably the most appropriate," I said. Instead of telling him what I knew, what I'd seen in my waking sleep.

"Yeah, good point."

"Okay, you start."

He was hesitating, though, just sitting there staring at the board.

"What's the matter?"

"I don't know."

"Do you want me to do it?"

"No, no."

"Are you scared?"

"It's not that, alright, Noelle?"

"Well what is it, Alf?"

"I don't know. I just, maybe we can try to contact my sister."

This I wasn't expecting. Alf hadn't brought up his sister again after that first time in the middle of the night when he'd told me about how she died. I didn't even know her name.

"We can try if you want to, Alf. But I don't really know how this works."

"What do you mean?"

"Well, like maybe we can only contact spirits who've died here, you know what I mean? And like, if we can contact any spirit anywhere, I don't know that we necessarily want to drag your sister to this place."

And I don't want to talk to your dead sister, Alf. I'm sorry, but I don't. I want to talk to Sybil. I want ask Sybil where the cats went, and whether or not Sammy's REALLY lying half-dead in the basement. I want to ask her what the house wants with me, why it keeps waking me up, why its permanent residents are always talking to me and whispering at me and maybe making me do terrible things to that poor cat.

"Yeah, okay. That makes sense."

"But hey, Alf, we can do whatever you want."

"Let's not, then. Let's not do it now. Or not here, in the suite."

"Okay. So you wanna try and contact Margaret then? Or Wink?"

"Sure," he sniffed. He was tearing up.

"Alf, what's the matter?"

"I just, for some reason for the past few nights, I just, I can't get her out of my head. I'm seeing her drowning again over and over and it just, I can't shake it. Even when I fall asleep it's all I dream about."[50]

"Well, fuck this then, let's just go back downstairs and play cards."

"No. No, I want to do this. It'll be fun, okay? I just, I wanna see something. It'll make me feel better if we see something. Honestly."

I nodded. And smiled, a massive smile so big and insane as to be infectious and finally it made Alf laugh.

We each placed the first two fingers of both hands on the planchette, as delicately as we could. Our backs straightened too because Ouija boards can always do that to a person. Maybe an involuntary gesture of respect for the dead.

"Okay, so, who do you want then?" he asked.

"I don't know, Alf, you're running this thing."

"Margaret, I guess?"

---

50 Because Alf never utilized his diary (we found it in a drawer in his room at the inn, empty), we weren't able to determine the nature or severity of these visions. Particularly whether or not they shared qualities with Noelle's own visions, or fugue states. According to Alf's parents and a few teachers and friends, he hadn't exhibited the kinds of outward changes that Noelle appeared to over the course of the summer.

"Better make sure your boner-hider's in place."

And he laughed and told me to shut up.

Then started his séance.

"We want to speak to the woman who lived here. The woman who was eaten."

"Why are you talking like that?"

"I don't know. It's solemn Ouija board talk. Haven't you ever seen a movie before?"

"Well, how is saying it like that more formal, or, like, more respectful than just saying Margaret?"

"Okay, this is what I'm talking about."

"What?"

"You're being so unpleasant! Would you just let me lead this thing?"

"Fine, cripes, don't let me kill your boner."

He rolled his eyes before continuing. "Margaret, we'd like to speak to you. Are you with us?"

Nothing happened. Nothing moved. There weren't even any sounds really, which was actually kind of weird for the inn, such an old creaky house with so many, even just regular bumps in the night, like pipes working in the walls, or wind rattling shutters, stuff like that. The conspicuous quiet I used to think was kind of funny, but hated now after last night.

"Alf, I don't think they're going to talk to you unless you free your boner."

"What?"

"Lose the pillow! They think you're a fat girl. They don't want to talk to you."

He flung the pillow at me. "There. Are you happy?"

I nodded.

Alf continued: "We want to speak to Margaret."

Silence.

"Margaret, if you're with us, please give us a sign."

"Okay okay okay, I'm sorry to interrupt again, but come on."

"What?!"

"Why do we ask for a sign? Like, why don't we ask them to use all of the signs on the goddamn Ouija board we're using, like fucking YES and fucking NO, instead of making us try to figure out the significance of some other random thing?"

And Alf burst out laughing and yelled, "FINE!" in fake exasperation.

"Okay! Margaret! Please, if you don't mind, whether with a candle flickering, lights turning off, a picture falling, or EVEN using this Ouija board, indicate to us that you're here."

Nothing. Nothing but the sound of a car passing outside. The tires on the road sounded rainy wet.

"Alfred, we don't have any candles lit," I said.

"Okay, genius. That's it," he said. "Why don't you lead the séance if you think you're so good at it."

"Hey, I didn't say I was even good at it. I'm just not an idiot."

We laughed and then I cleared my throat and we started again.

"Is Margaret in the room?" I asked.

And suddenly the planchette twitched and Alf and I both pulled our hands back at the same time, startled. I could see in his face he really hadn't done it, he hadn't moved a muscle, and I hadn't either, or so I thought. Maybe I'd had a little spasm in my finger or something. A spontaneous reflex, so small I could barely feel it.

We both kind of laughed some more.

"Did you do that?" Alf asked.

I shook my head and I knew he believed me too. Could tell just as well as I had been able to tell on him, that it was genuine fear and surprise that shook me when it moved.

"Do you wanna try again?" he asked.

I nodded.

We laid our fingers on it again.

And I repeated myself but it was a bit shaky. "Is Margaret in the room?"

And the planchette moved slowly, deliberately, that same slow deliberateness that moved the lantern in the closet under the stairs; that turned the knob and flicked off the lights. Whoever it was could be sitting with us and moving it with her cold dead fingers, right next to ours, invisible to us but visible to me when I dream. Maybe it was her. The floured woman. Sybil Groundwick. Died in this very room. Could she be sitting between us in that dark suite? The thought was making me sick but also excited. I wanted to press hard on my scalp but I didn't wanna move my fingers from the planchette, which now felt so alive.

It moved to the word NO.

Alf's eyes were massive. He chewed his bottom lip like a wad of bubblegum and stared at me. I looked up at him.

"Well," I continued, "who is this then?"

And it didn't move.

"Who's in the room with us?"

Again just the too-quiet of the suite, nothing moving, no lights flickering.

"Maybe," Alf whispered, "you can only ask it yes or no questions."

"Okay, okay. What should I ask?"

"I don't know. Try to find out who it is."

"Okay," I said, and sat straighter still and continued. "Are you a girl?"

And the planchette moved to the word YES.

"Are you a victim of Margaret and Wink?"

And the planchette quivered a bit but remained on the word YES.

And then I was sure. I knew exactly who it was.

It was Sybil. And she was sitting next to me. I could feel her weight, her pull, on the shared planchette on the board. I could even smell her floury skin, hear the sound of her severed throat gurgling.

"Are you from this town?"

And the planchette moved to the word NO.

"Where are you from?"

"Psst," whispered Alf, "only YES or NO questions!"

"Okay, okay. Um. Margaret's not in this room. Does she still live here at the inn?"

And the planchette moved to the word YES.

"Is she mad?"

And the planchette quivered but stayed on the word YES. And Alf looked at me, confused.

"What's she going to do to me?"

Again Alf started to correct me, tell me I was only supposed to ask it YES or NO questions, but he was interrupted when something ice-cold and wet washed suddenly across my feet and scared the living shit out of me. I leapt up and shrieked and Alf did too and we hugged each other and looked around wildly. I could feel his heart beating hard against my chest. And even though I was scared it still struck me as a nice feeling. Someone else's pumping blood. Someone else's rhythm against mine.

"What the fuck was that!" Alf screamed.

And my own heartbeat petered off, slowed back to normal as I saw that the wet ice-cold was my spilled coffee and not some cold dead claw wrapping around my toes.

"Christ. It was my coffee."

"Oh thank god."

And we caught our breath for a minute but Alf was still looking at me weird, confused.

"But what knocked it over?" he asked.

And I shivered and Alf did too. We both had our arms crossed and were gripping at our shoulders. I didn't say it out loud but I also wondered why the coffee felt so cold when just a few minutes ago it'd been piping hot.

"You knew who that was," he continued.

"What do you mean?"

"Who we were speaking to. You knew it was a girl, you knew it was a victim, you knew she wasn't from here. What's going on, Noelle? What do you think is gonna happen to you?"

"It's just common sense, Alf. If it's not Margaret and it's a girl, it must be a victim."

"Come on, don't be an asshole. Just tell me."

"What?"

"What did you see? You saw a ghost, I can tell, but you didn't tell me. That's why you were so scared to come up here tonight, that's why you've been so unpleasant lately."

And I really didn't want to. I really didn't. And usually, really, I don't, but this time it happened, I CRIED, and I absolutely hate to cry. But when I tried to lie all that came out of my mouth was a sputtering moan, then tears, filling up my eyes so fast, streaming down either side of my wide-open moaning mouth. This crying felt so ugly. I wish I'd have just told him the truth to begin with.

"Whoa, whoa, whoa, Noelle, what happened?"

"I don't know, Alf! I don't know!"

"Well, just, start from the beginning."

"I don't even know where that is!"

"Well, just, tell me something, Noelle, anything, because I'm feeling pretty fucking scared in here."

"I think that might have been Sybil Groundwick."

"Who?"

"The last one they killed, you remember her."

"The one, yeah, the one your dad said looked like she could eat, uh, what was it, corn on the cob through venetian blinds."

And I laughed because goddamnit I can't help laughing when I hear that. But it scared me too because making fun of the ghosts was violating a rule. [51]

"Yes, her."

---

51 Rule 4: Don't antagonize the ghosts.

I told him about seeing her. About what I found in my diary about hurting a cat, hurting Sammy, and then the next day all the cats were gone. About how real my dreams were. How there were OTHERS everywhere. And about how I tried to look in the basement, tried to go down the hallways but I couldn't because something held me back. I was so scared. And I told him about the light flicking off in the little closet and how something had spun the lantern and turned the knob on the door.

And I even told him about my dad. About how my dad was a fucking liar, how he hadn't been to a doctor in over a year and I just couldn't stop crying and crying and crying and telling and telling and telling Alf absolutely EVERYTHING.

Well, almost EVERYTHING. EVERYTHING except for the stuff about my head. He didn't need to know that. Even with EVERYTHING gushing out like it was, something still plugged that information in. Thank god.

And Alf just sat and listened. A big part of me was really hoping that he'd been experiencing something similar, that he'd seen a ghost, but he didn't say anything like that and I know he would have said so if he had.

After I was done he said, "Noelle, I promise, you didn't hurt Sammy."

"How can you promise that?"

"I just can. I know you didn't."

"But how do you know?"

"We're gonna go down to the basement, okay? And we're gonna look in all the rooms, and I promise we won't find a cat, okay?"

"No way, that's terrifying."

"Noelle, there's nothing down there. You and I both know, really, that there's no such thing as ghosts, okay? Yeah, we like to get scared, but we both know that. I also know that for whatever reason you're really upset right now, and I can make you less upset if I can prove to you that you didn't hurt any cat. I'm not scared. I'm really not."

"Well, if there's no ghosts, who moved the planchette then?"

"I have no idea. Maybe you did it."

"I did not!"

"Okay, maybe I did it."

"Did you?"

And Alf hesitated for a moment before he continued. "No," he said, "but listen, I don't give a shit. You didn't hurt that cat and I'm going to prove it to you. It's more important right now that you know you didn't hurt that cat, okay? Then we'll sleep all day and come in at night and have a great party, okay? I'll get Dwayne to get the beer because I know you were just about to ask that, who was gonna get the beer if I was sleeping all day."

And I laughed and I gave him a hug and then, without really thinking about it, a kiss on the lips too. And I know it made him really happy. And I felt happy too because Alf was sure of the fact that I would never maim a cat. So sure I wouldn't maim a cat that he'd even brave the basement at night. And not just any night, but a night like this, when we'd used the Ouija board in the suite and everything felt quiet and menacing and bad in here. And that made me feel like a really good person. Not Noelle the legendary asshole who hates her sick but not sick but actually sick father. But Noelle the person who would absolutely not hurt a cat. And someone else on earth was so sure of that fact that he'd chance potential death or maiming or pants-shitting in fear just to prove it.

He turned bright red again, especially his ears, and we packed up and headed downstairs.

Twenty-Second Entry

Even though Alf had claimed he wasn't scared, he still flicked the lights on and off five times before we went downstairs. And we still ran as fast as we could down those stairs. Because frankly, we were already doing something scary and stupid, descending into the basement in the middle of the night, about to enter one of the dark hallways. Why add to it by deliberately breaking all of these rules that'd served us so well for the whole summer so far?

I knew Alf was scared even though he told me he wasn't. Obviously. I'm not an idiot. But I also knew I needed to see if the cat was really there. I had to know. And he knew I had to know. This is why Alf is my very best friend.

We were about to break the eighth rule. [52]
We had to go down one of the hallways.

I knew which hallway I'd been led down in my dream. The seventh hallway, farthest from the staircase. Of course. Farthest from our only escape route.

Down that hallway, I hoped Sammy wasn't lying maimed.

Down that hallway, I hoped we wouldn't end up maimed.

"It's that one," I said, and pointed at it. And one single nail rolled across a metal shelf and landed with a pang on the concrete floor. The noises were starting, the little disturbances that occurred when people spent too long in the basement.

We ignored them.

The way we ignored them when we came down here to do laundry. But of course we weren't doing laundry now. We were breaking a rule.

Alf took my hand, held it tight, and began to lead me into the hallway's swallowing darkness.

Just before we entered the pitch black a thunderous clang make us both leap in fear,

---

52 Rule 8: Don't, under any circumstances, go down ANY of the basement hallways.

204

clutch one another like pieces of floating wood in the middle of an unfriendly ocean.

The pickaxe had fallen. On its side now, pointing at me.

"Jesus," whispered Alf.

And I couldn't stop shaking.

"Are you okay?" he asked.

And I nodded.

And we let ourselves get eaten up by the pitch blackness, our shaking flashlights forward. There was a door at the end of the tunnel, coated thick in chipping yellow paint. It seemed to keep inching farther away from us, the hallway impossibly long. Finally Alf was able to reach out and grab the knob. He tried to turn it but it wouldn't open.

"Locked," he whispered. And we both thought of rule five.[53]

"Try again," I whispered. "Bang into the door."

"What?"

"Like, bang into it with your shoulder. It works in movies."

And he turned the knob and slammed his whole body into the door, but again it wouldn't budge.

The noises continued in the main room,

---

53 Rule 5: Don't unlock locked doors.

louder now. And one particular noise that neither of us had ever heard down here before.

The sound of something dragging across the floor. Something heavy.

We both looked back, down the hall, towards the main room where the light was still on. We stared for a while but nothing appeared. We were both thinking of the same rule, I'm sure of it, that nothing can come out when the light is on. That's what we had decided, early on this summer.

But the dragging sound happened again.

Alf slammed himself harder and harder into the door.

"Are you sure it was this one?" he asked, winded.

"Positive. Okay, okay, let me try," I said.

I turned the knob and blasted all of my body weight into the door and it cracked open so easily I almost fell over inside.

"I guess you loosened it," I said, composing myself quickly in case there was anything bad in there.

And we moved our flashlights all over the room, terrified the light might catch something. A pair of cold, dead eyes, claw marks on the floor, bloody nails embedded in the walls. A maimed cat, yowling on the floor. But it was mostly empty.

Stained walls painted in the same careless, too-thick yellow paint. A bare mattress in one corner, thin with faint blue stripes. A bucket next to the mattress. The bucket. The bucket. That bucket couldn't be trusted. That bucket was bad. Bad like the pickaxe is bad. I should look inside the bucket. I should look inside the bucket and show Alf what was in there, show him what I did. Showing is so different from just telling while crying and being all weak and scared and pretty, telling him something that made him feel like he could be a hero. But I didn't want to show him. Not now after I'd kissed him. Things were different now, goddammit. Diary, I couldn't. You don't understand. Now that we were there I couldn't show him. I couldn't do it.

And the dragging outside got louder. Louder. Louder. Whatever was being dragged was being dragged closer to us.

But actually there couldn't be anything in that bucket. That bucket was fine. It was too small to fit a cat. And it was in the wrong spot, way on the other side of the room, nowhere near where patterned-space Sammy had wheezed. And in my dreams there was blood all over the floor; in real life this floor was just dusty. So it's okay. There's nothing wrong with it. There's nothing wrong with anything here. I get the same kind of chills from that stupid pickaxe too, for no good reason at all. Nothing to worry about. Okay? Tell me I'm right, diary. Or I'll lock you down here. I'm sorry, no I won't.

"Nothing!" Alf said, and forced a big smile. "See? I knew you couldn't hurt that cat, Noelle. You'd never do anything like that, okay? Are you satisfied?"

But I had to know. We'd come all the way down here. I had to see.

So I laid my flashlight over the bucket.

"There won't be anything in there, Noelle. It's too small for a cat. Plus there's no blood on the floor. It couldn't be like how you described it."

And Alf kept saying all the things I was thinking. You're crazy, Noelle. Don't trust yourself. There's nothing in there. Nothing to worry about. NO CAT! This is great news! NO CAT, no blood on the floor. This wasn't at all how it looked at night, guided down here by the floured woman.

But then where is Sammy? Where are the rest of the cats? Shut up, diary. SHUT UP. SHUT UP! SHUT UP!

I kept the flashlight on the bucket, not convinced, goddammit, not convinced even though I was trying so hard. And I didn't want Alf to see but I couldn't look, I couldn't look.

So I whispered, "I can't look."

"That's okay," said Alf, but his voice cracked. And it took a minute of him squeezing fists at his sides before he was able to slowly walk towards the bucket, my flashlight's shaking beam overtop of it as he peered inside.

"He's not here!" he declared, obviously very relieved not to have discovered a maimed cat. "He's not in here, Noelle!"

And I felt so happy I almost cried, I smiled so wide, and Alf came back and hugged me, and I felt his heart beating against me again and it was just so nice.

"Is it empty?" I asked.

"Yeah, just some old garbage," he said.

So relieved. So very, actually, completely relieved. There was no dying cat down here. There really wasn't. That's all I wanted to know, and now I knew. The end.

"Now, let's get the fuck out of here," said Alf.

And we turned to get the fuck out.

And found a big, fat, dark figure at the end of the hall, breaking apart the main room's unnatural light, blocking our only exit. My heart tried to escape through my throat. I think Alfred might have pissed his pants. I pulled him into the room and slammed the door shut behind us.

And that's where we're stuck now. I'm using the flashlight to write in here.

Alf did piss his pants.

We tried to listen through the door for a while but couldn't hear anything. Even all the little basement noises had stopped. No more nails rolling off shelves, things falling to the ground. Like the basement was settled now. Like we belonged in here.

Both of us were too scared to open the door again.

We decided to wait until the morning, when Jessica arrives. We'll be able to hear her walking to the front desk through the floor. It'll be morning, sunlight coming in through the cats' window. Everything will be better then.

So until then we're gonna try and sleep.

But it's hard with that something still out there. Waiting. Maybe just on the other side of the door, head pressed against the cold yellow paint, listening just like we are, ready to grab us as soon as we open it.

Twenty-Third Entry

Awake now next to Alf. We're on the floor with our sweaters balled up beneath our heads. He has his arm around me even though he never asked if he could do that and his pants are all pissy. But I guess it's fine.

She's here too. Sitting cross-legged on the mattress in the corner, staring at the wall so I can only see the back of her. Her dress is pulled up, thin thighs like rolled dough. Floury white. I want to slice them into biscuits, watch them rise in an oven. Her back moves as though her hands are busy.

And Sammy lies on the floor behind her, the way he was before, still breathing somehow, blood everywhere. I get up and walk towards him. I reach into the bucket that'd been next to the bed yesterday but is now at Sammy's side.

His food and his water, hidden beneath some old newspapers I'd found. I feed him a bit and dribble more water into his mouth, furry chin barely moving.

"We have to hide him," says the floured woman.

Says Sibyl. Says Sibyl Groundwick. Says dead Sibyl Groundwick.

"You know he's not allowed to see," she continues and nods toward a sleeping Alf.

"But why?"

"Because then he'll know. And he won't wanna come back here."

"Right."

"Trust me, you don't wanna be here all alone."

"I know."

"Pick up your baby."

So I very delicately lift Sammy, wrap him in my sweater, his breathing rasping harder and faster, his throat wants to close and end the misery.

And I rock him back and forth and back and forth. I know I need to kill him. So I stroke his little face and it suddenly looks like a real little baby's face. A little baby born and died, eyes like scoops of jelly in his little baby skull. I need to kill this baby. Because this isn't a life. I need to kill it, the way that they should have killed me. Stupid Roberta and stupid fucking Herman.

I hate you, Herman. I hate you. I hate you for wishing me to life, you had no right goddamn you.

And I grab Sammy's little throat and Sibyl says, "Don't hurt the baby..." in a high-pitched voice, too soft. It makes me sick so I gag and think it should wake me up to gag but it doesn't. And suddenly I can picture her soggy rotting dead throat so well, air passing through it, grating, pulling bits of her stinking flesh away with it, splatting against my cheek.

I press harder.

"Don't, please," says Sibyl. "Please don't do it. Margaret will be very angry and we don't wanna see her angry, please oh please oh please!" — Or she'll send her criminally insane son to kill you!

And Sybil is shaking, flour puffing off of her skin.

"What do you care?" I ask.

"You don't know what she can do."

"But I can't let him live like this!"

"Margaret says babies are precious."

"She's a murderer!"

"No. He was a murderer. He was a murderer. Not Margaret. Not Margaret. Not Margaret. Margaret says. Margaret says she opened me up but didn't kill me."

I have to kill him. I have to. He's trapped in

a living hell. And I'm the one who trapped him,
like Herman trapped me. I can't be like Herman,
I can't do this to Sammy. Then I dig my finger so
hard into my scalp I think I feel my skull and it
burns like fuck but it feels so good, like I'm grow-
ing somehow. Like this pain is progress.

And I squeeze Sammy's little throat shut,
harder and harder as I dig harder and harder into
my head and he rattles with gratitude. And Sibyl
is going wild in the corner of my eye, terrified but
also excited, screaming but I can't quite hear.

And I squeeze harder and harder but just
before I feel the life leave little Sammy's body
I suddenly hear a loud BANG BANG BANG
BANG BANG BANG BANG at the door.
Dust explodes in puffs from the old hinges.

"Oh no no no no no no no no no!" Sibyl
moans, sadness and terror mixed together. Alf is
still sound asleep on the floor.

"What?"

"No no no no no no no no no no," and she
clawed at her hair and groaned.

"What is it?"

"Margaret."

"Margaret?"

"Margaret is going to be very upset. She
doesn't like how you're trying to kill this little
baby. You better run. Run away. Don't ever
come back if you can get away."

"But I didn't kill him! I didn't, see?" and I thrust out Sammy for her to look. "He's not dead!"

And then Margaret pounds again.

Sybil gets up and walks over to the door.

"Don't…" I say. "Look, he's not dead, you don't have to do this!"

"I have to let her in."

"Please, no!"

"I have to or she'll punish me."

Sybil flings open the door and something massive and hot and powerful comes tumbling in and without thinking I drop Sammy's still barely breathing body to the floor, the sound of his skull cracking on the ground, and then I plough through it, her, the big fat thing blocking our way, and I run for my life, and it follows me up the stairs, pounding pounding pounding, grunting, cold fingers just barely getting me but I can feel them and I might be screaming. And I escape out the front door and run run run for my life some more. Fuck you, Herman. Fuck you for wishing me to life. Run run run run run.

I'm going to show you. You lying piece of shit.

I'm going to show you why you should have killed me when you had the chance. [54]

---

54 This section takes up 18 pages in the diary.

Twenty-Fourth Entry

I woke up in the basement, outside the closed door at the end of the dark hallway. My hands gloved to the elbows in thick dry blood, my head throbbing, hair stiff as spider legs, the ache in my head so powerful I didn't know what to do. I'd really gone to town on my sore spot. Fuck. My shoes were covered in mud. I must have been outside.

Alf couldn't see me this way. I had to hide all the blood on my face, rub the mud off my shoes. I went over to the laundry sink and rinsed my hands, filled the basin almost to the top with cold water and dunked my head in. Eyes open I let myself drift into patterned space for as long as I could, hair swirling slow around my face. I held my breath for so long

I thought my eyeballs were going to pop out but it felt good. It was relaxing me.

I dried myself off and snuck back into the room and read the last few pages of the diary. As I read them I felt as though all my bones were slowly fusing together, fused and frozen that way. I'd never be able to move again.

Sammy's not here again now. So that stuff must not be real. But it feels so real. Oh god, maybe I'm crazy like Herman.

But the other cats really are gone. They've been gone for days. So maybe it's the house that scared them away. Maybe it's the house that's making me see things.

And really, if it's the house, everything's fine. Really. When you think about it. Because at least I'm not crazy. And all that's happening, I guess, is that the ghosts are tormenting me? Or trying to show me something? In movies ghosts always have some motive, to solve their murders or, like, dig up their bodies and put them to rest in consecrated ground. There aren't really any unsolved mysteries here though. I think the house is just a fucking asshole.

But anyway, the most important thing is, there's no cat here slowly dying. And you know what? I don't think a cat could possibly survive being half-smashed for as long as

Sammy's been apparently half-smashed. So this is all bullshit.

It doesn't matter.

"Keep it coming!" I whispered out loud to Margaret or Sybil or whoever was down here. And I meant it too. I wanted to see what else they would show me. If this was all they had to torture me they'd severely underestimated the hell I'd already been living in my whole life.

Alf was still sleeping. I would pretend that I didn't leave him here. I can't believe I did. At first I thought I was so lucky that whatever that hulking thing was didn't fucking kill him. But now I think she probably couldn't have if she tried. Big fat Margaret.

"Big fat Margaret," again out loud because I'm not scared anymore. She can't hurt us. Big fat ugly Margaret, all she can do is stomp around with her stupid red toenails, and the only people she can hurt, I guess, are the people she's already killed. Like poor Sybil.

I guess she did hurt me once, when I was sleepwalking. She rammed her finger too hard into my sore head and then the diary entry ended. But I don't remember it, I don't remember the pain. Diary, maybe you just wrote it in there so that I'd feel scared of her. Probably she didn't hurt me at all. Right?

Am I right, diary? Does any of this make sense?

They can't hurt me. Or Alf.

Tell me, diary. TELL ME!

Whose side are you on anyway? Are you working with her, you dick? Don't forget I'm your mother and your father. So you've gotta do whatever I say, otherwise I'll cripple you with guilt.

So much gore beneath my nails. So much digging in my head. It hurt so bad today and it felt hot and sticky under my fingers. Sticky hot syrup. A smooth spot in the middle. Maybe my skull. My skull? Is that really possible?

I didn't wanna look at it.

My face was buried in the dairy, reading and re-reading when Alf spoke and startled me.

"Hey," he said. He was sitting up. Pale as paper. "Why is your hair all wet?" He sounded so serious.

"I—I—" I started. I'd forgotten to come up with a lie for this.

"Your hair is wet, Noelle. Your hair is wet. Did you? No. I can't even say it because if it's true I'll kill you. Did you fucking LEAVE ME DOWN HERE alone in the goddamn basement to take a shower?"

"No! No I swear I didn't. I just, I rinsed my hair a bit in the, in the laundry sink because it's just really dirty down here."

I had no idea what else to say. He still wouldn't like that. That I'd left him alone in here at all. But I'd rather admit to that than admit to having woken up in the hallway covered in blood from my own ravaged head, with no memory of how I got there, a new fucked-up entry in my diary.

"Um, really? Is it dirty down here? And scary and terrible? I hadn't noticed!"

"You—just—looked—so—peaceful! I didn't want to disturb you, we'd had such a crazy night, I just—"

"Noelle, I don't even know what to say. You left me in a dangerous haunted basement room all alone. You're the fucking WORST!"

"I'm sorry! Alfred, I'm sorry, please don't be mad at me. I just, I'm an idiot, I fucked up. I didn't think it was as scary during the day, but I'm a fool."

"I'm going home."

"Okay, yes, go home, sleep."

"I don't think I can come back tonight."

"Alfred, you have to! It's the party!"

"Yeah, I know it's the party, Noelle. I'm just, I don't know what to think about last night."

"Alf, please! Come on. We knew that something like this might happen. We both knew this coming into the job. Last night you were all about this. Last night you wanted something like this to happen. You took a goddamn Ouija board into the suite for christsake! I'm the one who told you not to!"

"Oh, fuck you, Noelle, you left me down a goddamn hallway!"

Then we stood there for a minute.

"Aren't you going to storm out?" I asked.

"I don't wanna go alone."

"Aw, Alf. Please don't be mad at me. I'm an idiot, I'm a jerk, I'm sorry. Okay, how about this. I'll go get the beer for tonight. I'll go. Okay?"

"Um, Noelle, I don't think you get it. I pissed my fucking pants last night. In terror. That's never happened to me before."

"So you're just going to leave me alone with the party tonight?"

"Let's just cancel it!"

"Yeah, cancel it, that's gonna look REALLY cool. Everyone will hate us, Alf!"

"Oh, they will not."

"They will too!"

"Well, who cares?"

"You want to tell a group of high school kids in this town that the reason we can't throw the most terrifying Anniversary party of all time in the most perfect place for it is because we actually literally SAW a ghost? Maybe saw fucking Margaret? Who the Anniversary is FOR in the first place?"

And I could see his shoulders slump. It was a stupid reason to do something that you think might be scary and dangerous, yeah. Really stupid. But bad reputations are as real as ghosts.

"I'm scared, Noelle."

"It'll be fine, okay? Nothing really even happened last night."

"What the hell are you talking about?"

"Well, before we saw that person, that figure or whatever, nothing really happened, right?"

"No, lots of things happened. The Ouija board, all that stuff you told me about."

"Okay, fine, but like, as it turns out, there's no cat down here, right? So that stuff wasn't true. And really, nothing *hurt* us. It probably couldn't hurt us if it wanted to."

"What do you mean?"

"What I mean is, this house is just, it's got a lot of impressions on it, I guess, from being so old and having so much happen here, right? That doesn't mean that those, those impressions, that doesn't mean that they can hurt you. Nothing happened last night, and maybe it could have, but it didn't. Which makes me think that maybe nothing CAN actually happen. Do you know what I mean? We were safe in here, nothing got in. Maybe that's because they're not that powerful, you know? Or not powerful at all. Just scary. We're really lucky, Alf. We saw a real live ghost, okay? Isn't that pretty amazing?"

"I guess that's true. Nothing really happened. Except that it was fucking scary."

"Exactly, and honestly, we wanted to get scared last night. You did, remember? Alf, you wanted to see something. You said it would make you feel better."

I'm rotten, I'm rotten and evil bringing up his sister like that, but I kept going. "Would you just"—and I grabbed his hands—"think about it? Think about coming tonight? This could honestly be the best Anniversary party of all time. I know you'll regret missing it."

And he held my hands tight. They were so cold and shaking. I felt like an asshole. Why was I making him do this? I didn't even wanna come back here. Ever again. Sybil told me to run away and keep running. Who decides not to heed the warning of a goddamn ghost? And why would I keep coming back to a house that was trying to torture me? It's crazy and stupid and definitely dangerous. I don't wanna come back. I don't wanna come back. But that isn't true. I'm writing it but it isn't true. Something in me wants to come back. Something in me never wants to leave.

What will the house do next, diary? What is it really capable of? You better tell me, diary. Otherwise I'll send you to bed without dinner. I'll lock you in the closet and make you think about what you've done. I'll spank you. I'll kill you.

I led Alf slowly out of the basement, then out the front door and we walked the part of the walk home that we shared.

When it was time to part ways, I asked, "Do you want me to walk you home?"

"No, I'm fine."

"I'll get the beers, okay?"

"Okay."

"You just sleep."

And I leaned in and I kissed him again. Slow on the mouth. And I liked it. It felt good. I didn't want to upset Alf and I didn't want this to have happened this way. But I wanted him to come tonight. And this is the way to get boys to do what you want. Because they're stupid.

Twenty-Fifth Entry

When I got home the chair in the living room was empty, which meant that my father was still sleeping.

And usually I wouldn't do this, but this morning I felt the need to go up to his room to make sure. Make sure he was there, in bed, and make sure he was sleeping and not, you know. I don't know.

He was there. A big fat lump under the cheap covers. I didn't want to get too close. Close enough that he feels someone lingering around and wakes up and then I have to talk to him.

I felt relieved but also kind of disappointed. But I don't want to tell you why, diary.

No.

No no no.

Why do you want to know so bad? What difference does it make?

I'm sure you can guess, okay? I'm sure you know why I felt that way.

Because! Jesus. I can't believe you're making me write this down. You're a fool. If I go down, you're going down with me, you know that? I shouldn't write this down in here.

Okay, okay. I thought maybe, from what I wrote, what I wrote when I was sleepwalking or whatever, I thought that I'd maybe... that I'd killed Herman. That I ran home here and killed him.

And I know this is terrible but when I thought he might be dead and finally out of my life for good, it made me feel really relieved, okay? I was hoping sort of (BUT NOT REALLY) that when I came in there would be a carcass arranged in an undeniably DEAD way in the center of a glistening red pool of way more blood than I'd ever seen in my life.

But no. Here he is. Big lazy sleeping lump. Who'd never know what hit him if his throat just started closing in his sleep.

I don't want him dead, okay diary? So stop making me write that stuff down.

I groped around in his disgusting bag for the keys to the car, found them, and drove it into the next town over to buy Alf and me more beer than we could ever drink in a night.

Then I drove around and around until there was almost no gas left and I came home and slipped the keys back into his nasty bag and couldn't wait for him to discover the empty tank. It was very important to Herman that I got my license as soon as I possibly could. So I could run even more errands for him, pick up food within a much larger radius. Fucking asshole jerkface.

I don't know when he'll be using the car again though. It's not like he's visiting Dr. Schiller. Goddamn fucking liar.

I called Alf's house. His mom said he was sleeping. That's good. He should sleep.

I'm going to try and sleep too.

Twenty-Sixth Entry

Right now I'm sitting at the front desk and I have no idea if Alf is going to show up or not. He never called me back.

Olivia is sitting in one of the chairs with no arms and she's started on a coughing fit that's lasting for goddamn ever. I'm actually a little worried she's going to keel over and die. But she probably won't.

The door just opened. A customer? A goddamn customer on tonight of all nights?!

Even Olivia looked nervous. I think she wanted Alf and me to be able to have our "dinner," to be able to hang out with our friends one night this summer. I haven't seen June or Andrea, or anyone else from school, in forever. Just Alf. Alf all the time. Olivia really does care about us. She really does want us to be happy.

But it wasn't a customer. It was Alf. Good old Alf.

"Hi," he said quietly.

"Alf!"

"I knew you wouldn't cancel the party," he whispered so Olivia couldn't hear.

"Of course not."

"And I couldn't let you do this all alone."

"Thanks, man."

And we hugged and it felt nice but I sort of felt bad about kissing him before, because even though maybe I do like Alf that way, I only kissed him to get him to show up tonight, and he did, and now I felt gross about it.

"You look different," I said.

He was wearing jeans instead of sweatpants. And he'd combed his hair differently, so he didn't look like a pervert anymore.

"Oh yeah, I bought these pants a little while ago." And he twirled around in a very Alf way.

"I like them."

"Thanks."

Olivia walked up to the front desk. She was sweating from her coughing fit.

"Alright, you two, I'm leaving now." Her meter was close to the top.

"Okay," Alf said.

"How come you were late?" she asked Alf. She wasn't angry. Just curious.

"I guess I slept in," he replied.

"Well, it looks to me like you were primping for your dinner! You look very sharp, Alfred."

"Thanks, Olivia." He blushed. And somehow he didn't blurt some long, inappropriate story about grooming his pubes or something.

"It's a good thing we didn't get any of those novelty guests in, hmm?" Olivia said as she put on her coat.

"Yeah, well, I think most people outside of town have kinda forgot about it by now," I said.

"You know, I remember a time when this was the busiest night of the year. A bunch of freaks wanting to stir up trouble in here."

"Well, I'm glad it stopped," said Alf. Even though we were exactly a pair of freaks trying to stir up trouble.

"Me too." And Olivia smiled and said, "Alright, well, you guys don't make a mess, okay? And you know, it's okay by me if you decide to have a few drinks and all, and really I'd rather you do it here than outside somewhere, but please don't let anyone drive drunk or anything like that. And don't let anyone puke anywhere."

"We won't," I said.

"And you know, if you make a mess, you'll be the ones who'll have to clean it all up."

"Well, and you asked us not to make a mess. We listen to you sometimes too, Olivia."

And she laughed. And repeated again, begged us, really, not to make a mess. And then finally left. I felt a little bad that we were about to throw a giant party.

"Thanks for coming, Alf."

"Yeah, yeah, stop thanking me."

"No, really though."

"Well, I just figured, like, you're right. Probably nothing's going to happen tonight. Nothing like that would ever happen with so many people around."

"It's true, you know."

"And nothing *really* happened yesterday. I mean, it was scary and all, but I mean, neither of us was hurt. It was actually pretty exciting."

"Right? I think tonight's gonna be a blast."

"Is there coffee?" asked Alf.

"Yep. Wanna play cards?"

"Sure. Okay, lemme get coffee, then we can play."

It was hot in here. Too hot. I took the

cards out of the cupboard and went over to the thermostat. Someone had turned off the air conditioner. Who the hell would do that? Certainly not Olivia. I'm pretty sure I didn't do it either. Pretty sure.

Alf emerged from the kitchen, talking.

"Noelle, if we end being murdered by ghosts and this is our last night together, I just want you to know something."

"What?"

"I want you to know that … ugh man, okay, I want you to know that I … I saw your boob once."

"Alfred, you bastard! When was that?"

"That time we were both up watching that movie about the lawyer and the criminal and he like, goes after the guy's family. The one in black and white."

"Oh yeah, yeah. Cape Fear."

"Yeah, that one."

"How did you see my boob that night?"

Alf's shoulders moved up slowly and touched his ears before he continued. "Well, remember how it was your turn to close the window? Because I always have to do it." I started to interject but he cut me off. "And don't even start, Noelle, you know I always have to do it." I shut up because he was right. "Well, when you got up to spin the closer thing, I could see up your shirt and I saw your boob and I'm sorry. I couldn't potentially go to my grave tonight without you knowing."

"Alright. You know what? Thanks for coming out about it. Now you get to die feeling good about yourself and I get to die feeling violated and disgusted."

"Haha, hey!" and he kinda punched my shoulder the way that he had been all summer. Because of his goddamn annoying crush. But it didn't feel annoying this time.

"Well I should come clean about something too," I said. "Remember when you got your learner's permit?"

"Yeah."

"And you'd been saving that Coke all night for, like, a caffeine boost right before you left?"

"Yeah."

"I'm the one who drank it."

"Um, yeah, Noelle, I fucking knew you did!"

"How did you know?"

"There was no one else there that night! It had to have been you. And you just lied and lied and lied."

"Yeah, yeah well. I'm telling you now."

"Well. Thank you. Because it was really annoying you wouldn't just tell the truth."

"Well, it could have been the guest!"

"What guest?"

"We had a guest that night. She could have easily opened up the fridge and taken it."

"No we didn't!"

"Yes we did, Alf. I talked to her for, like, half an hour about drinking your stupid Coke. I felt terrible about it."

"Hey, Noelle, we absolutely did not have a guest. I remember because it's one of the reasons I found your lying so funny, that like, there was literally NO ONE ELSE who could have taken it."

"Yes, we did too have a guest. That fat lady, she was maybe, I don't know, twenty or thirty. Really ugly. Really fat. Come on, you checked her in!"

"NOELLE! I seriously didn't!"

"She said you checked her in."

"Noelle, I'm telling you, I didn't check in any lady before my driver's test."

"Okay, fine then. Let's check the system."

"Okay, let's."

I went to the computer and turned it on.

"When was your test?"

"July 18th."

I clicked through the calendar to July 17th. And it was empty. We didn't have any guests that night.

And Alf and I got very quiet then, because we both realized what this meant.

That I had seen a ghost almost right away. Almost as soon as the summer started. And Alf wondered if maybe he had too.

We thought of all of them, the old man on the low calorie diet, the strange woman with the birdcage.

And there had been others. OTHERS. [55] Not many. But enough to make me feel cold despite the fact that the air conditioning hadn't kicked in yet.

"You said she was fat?" asked Alf.

I nodded. I knew what he was thinking. That maybe it'd been Margaret. Big fat Margaret, and I'd spoken to her. She'd told me Alf wouldn't be mad about the Coke, that Alf would have let me drink it if I'd asked. I remembered her smile, teeth glazed in saliva, reflecting the lobby's bright light. She wore

---

55 We're currently going through the guest history for the past three months, locating the guests we're able to and asking them to sit for interviews about their stay: strange phenomena, odd behaviors from either Noelle or Alf, suspicious-looking persons on the premises, etc. There are a large number of guest who we haven't been able to locate.

slippers, which seemed odd, but not so odd I thought she might be a fucking ghost. Had I seen her feet? Did she have red toenails? I can't remember. She looked so alive. She was sweating, for god's sake.

And I realized then that the house wasn't the most quiet on the nights we had guests. It was louder than ever those nights, showing itself to us as hard as it could.

I started dealing out the cards. But I dealt too many and had to start again. Twice. We were both quiet for a while as we played.

Until finally Alf spoke, probably as tired of his own thoughts as I was. "So, uh, how's your dad?" he asked.

And for some reason my throat felt too clogged up to answer right away. "He's still a liar." I cleared it. "Why?"

"Well, I've been here for, like, an hour and he hasn't called fifty times."

"That's true, actually. Well, I think he's not feeling so well right now. When I left tonight he was sleeping."

"I thought he was feeling better. Or whatever it is. I thought the chicken made him think he was cured."

"Um, he was, I guess. But then he went out to buy himself another chicken and apparently it was a goddamn disaster."

"Sorry, man."

"Yeah, it's alright."

And we continued to play cards for a long time before we started setting up for the party.

Twenty-Seventh Entry

People have started showing up. Like, already twenty at least. Or maybe thirty. Who knows. I'm bad at that kind of thing. I don't even know how many people to expect. Alf probably does.

I'm leaving you in the closet, diary. I hope it's not too dark and scary in here for you. Now that you're alive and all.

Getting drunk is weird, like, deliberately making yourself a retard. Spending money even, and going out of your way to, like, temporarily disable yourself.

And yet it's somehow worth it. This crazy thing that people love but are also scared of. Especially girls. A lot of girls hate the feeling of being retarded and disabled and out of control.

To a lot of girls at my school being TOO DRUNK can be this very shameful thing. I guess because when girls are out of control, like the way you are when you're drunk, you get blamed for the stuff that happens to you, whereas guys just kind of get to laugh about how drunk they can get.

TOO DRUNK. YOU'RE A GIRL WHO GETS DRUNK. TOO DRUNK. And to some other kind of a girl that means you're a girl who deserves what she gets.

One time June dumped a beer on a girl for saying that to her, that she was TOO DRUNK. It was crazy, but also great.

I guess we're all like that, June and Andrea and me, we all don't mind that feeling of being out of control, will keep going and going and going till we're snoring bubbles into our own puke. And that's one of the reasons we're friends.

Andrea is probably the prettiest of the three of us. She'd probably say that I was but actually secretly think it's her. Because that's what I just did.

June's good-looking too but sort of bigger, always kinda dieting. But verging on something scarier.

Because sometimes she's "a little bit bulimic." Which she's somehow got me convinced is really possible, that a person can be just "a little bit bulimic." And that actually, having that kind of control over your gag reflex is a handy skill.

Anyway, she said that as soon as she has enough money for a gym membership, she'll stop and I believe it for some reason.

Andrea has a gym membership, she goes a lot.

I'm too lazy for an eating disorder or a gym membership.

June's mom caught her puking and made her speak to a therapist. Today was her first session so Andrea and I asked her how it went. Because we're her BEST FRIENDS, so we've gotta ask things like that.

"She said I've got body dysmorphic disorder," June revealed.

"What's that?" asked Andrea.

"It's like, when you don't see how you really look in the mirror, right?" I asked. [56]

"Yeah, that's it. Like, what I'm seeing isn't actually how I look because my brain is putting, like, an ugly filter on it."

"Oh, well, your ugly filter must be on all of our brains," said Andrea.

---

56 A body-image disorder characterized by insidious negative thoughts about a minor or often imagined defect in appearance.

"You're so mean!" And June slapped her arm.

Alf came over and brought us all beers. The Alfred in him was really coming out as the host of the party.

"Thanks!" I said.

They just smiled. June and Andrea didn't quite know what to make of Alf yet. Like, to them Alf was this kind of weird guy I worked with who also apparently went to our school but they didn't recognize him. I'd barely talked to them all summer so they had no idea that actually Alf had become my very best friend, and that we'd kissed, and that he had a terrible crush on me. Not that I would have necessarily told them that anyway, even if all my time hadn't been hijacked by the nightshift.

On the outside Alf is sort of a boring nice-guy type. I didn't really know what to make of him either, at first. He doesn't come off as particularly smart or funny or cool or good-looking until you really get to know him, but then you can see that he really is funny and smart and cool and good-looking underneath all his stupid clothes and shyness. He just makes it really hard to get there.

Alf and I are going to be best friends for-ever.

Okay, that is officially the most embar-rassing thing I've written in this whole diary.

As he passed me my beer he smiled at me but his smile was sort of cracked down the middle. And I think that was fear. Good old Alf. Good old sweet nice Alf who could save me, he could. He could save me from the house and the things that live here. I wish there was some kind of black light, like cops use to find semen and blood and guts, that worked for seeing ghosts; for seeing spirit stains. So I could be more in control when Sibyl came out. When Margaret appeared to scold me. Because I'd made her upset. According to you, diary, Margaret is very mad at me.

"Are you okay?" asked June.

I must have zoned out.

"Yeah, go on. Go on about the session," I said.

"Well anyway, the therapist told me I had that body dysmorphia thing. But I think she's full of shit."

"You don't think you have it?"

"Fuck no. I'm fucking fat. I know I am. I wish it was goddamn body dysmorphia," and she took a big glug of beer. The kind that makes you wanna take a drink too, so I did. Seeing someone take a really refreshing-looking drink of something, especially beer, is just as contagious as a yawn.

"Oh goddammit, June, you're not fat." Andrea grabbed her shoulders and pulled her close into a hug. Squeezing her too tight, so June squirmed and pushed Andrea off of her.

"Anyway, stop worrying," said June. "Hopefully I am body dysmorphic."

"Yeah, fingers crossed you've got a crippling mental condition!" Andrea laughed.

I laughed too, then excused myself to find Alf.

"Hey." I grabbed his arm. He was filling up bowls of chips, just like an Alf.

"Hi," he said.

"Are you okay?"

"I'm fine."

"You look all freaked out."

"No, I'm fine. I just, I have kind of a weird feeling."

"Like what?"

"I don't know."

"Are you worried about"—I whispered lower—"are you worried about ghosts?"

"No, no. Well, I don't know, I guess that's part of it, yeah."

"Alf, don't worry about it. We're gonna be

fine. I promise. And nothing can really happen anyway, remember? They can't hurt us."

"I know, I know. I'm fine."

I went over to the big table we'd pushed against the far wall and grabbed a bottle of whiskey. I don't know who it belonged to but it didn't really matter because we were hosting the party so we got to drink whatever we wanted.

I opened it up and took a big swig of it. It burned and I couldn't twist my face hard enough to make it stop.

"Here," and I held it out to Alf, who was laughing at my twisted face.

"You make it look so delicious!" he said.

"Just drink it, Alf."

And he did.

"Feel better?"

"Actually yeah!" he said.

And we kept drinking the whiskey till there wasn't much left.

Twenty-Eighth Entry

Okay back again. The good thing about The Boy Eats Girl Inn is that all the carpets and the furniture are so goddamn gaudy that even if someone happened to spill the most stainable substance on anything, Olivia would probably never even notice.

I'm kinda drunk. Kinda drunk. Okay I'm pretty drunk. The first sign of drunkenness is terribly underestimating your drunkenness. Body getting all slow and dumb.

There are lots of people here now. Probably too many. Probably we're really going to regret having invited absolutely everyone from school to this party, but right now I don't care.

I'm hiding in the closet. Everything's going great. Everyone's having fun. There's this idiot here named Bill. He said the dumbest fucking thing I've ever heard in my life. He was trying to hit on Andrea and noticed that she bites her nails and he said, "You know girls who bite their nails are sub-consciously lesbians. Did you know that? Think about it... yeah."

Right? He's one of the dumbest people in the world.

But I'm pretty sure Andrea is going to sleep with him. Because he's really good-looking and if people find out she slept with him, they'll maybe bump her up a level in attractiveness.

Actually THAT'S the dumbest fucking thing in the world. But it's true. She'll prob-ably look a tiny bit hotter to everyone if she bangs him. Even to me. God, we should all be aborted.

Diary, I really hope you're planning to kill me; kill all of us; put us out of our misery.

Oh shit, someone fell down the stairs. Christ that's loud under here. [57]

Okay it sounds like they're fine.

Dwayne showed up even though no one ended up using him for booze. I don't know how he found out about it, but whatever.

---

57 In the closet under the stairs.

Turns out it was his whiskey that Alf and I took so he isn't as tremendously drunk as usual, but he'll get there soon. Last I saw him he was swaying by himself in front of a speaker, with a look on his face like he'd just swallowed a live goldfish.

Why is everyone even here? Clothes better than usual, hair better than usual, faces better than usual. They can't just be here to get drunk, surely. There were lots of basements and parking lots and jungle gyms and schoolyards for that. So what? They're here so they can all be like you, diary. Or I guess, like me through you. They all wanna work on a better version of themselves by showing up and hanging out and acting a certain way. They're all a bunch of walking diaries. You're as real as they are. And you are too because I made you real. I wished you to life, remember?

Of course you remember. Because apparently that was the single BEST thing that's ever happened to you in your life. BEING BORN. BEING BORN. YOU'RE SO LUCKY FOR BEING BORN. Be grateful to me, diary, because I gave you the most precious gift, right?

I hope you don't mind being stuck here in the closet in the dark all night. I'm not trying to punish you, it's just that I don't have any big pockets on right now, and I can't let anyone find you. This is where you've gotta stay so I can come in and take breaks with you, write stuff down in the most flattering way I can so I don't forget it. Because you're the better, more flattering version of me, remember? And you're alive, so pretty soon I really am going to have to start hating you.

Speaking of hatred. There is a girl here tonight, this girl named Robin, who one of Alf's friends brought to meet him. Alf's friend (Ian) thought that she and Alf would "hit it off" which made me more angry than I thought it would. And I was extra angry because it turns out Alf knew Ian would be bringing her, so he combed his hair and wore jeans instead of sweatpants.

I thought maybe he'd worn them because of our kiss.

Okay, diary, you're right, he did wear them because of our kiss, okay? Okay, shut up.

Robin's got an okay body and is pretty. Pretty in the way that missing or murdered girls are pretty. That wholesome kind of "this girl was going to grow up and be a hot mom one day" way and now she won't have babies and be a boring member of society like the rest of us because something killed her too soon. TOO SOON. Whatever that means. Too soon.

I hate Robin.

Alf and I can't be friends forever if I hate all of the girls who might wanna date him as much as I hate Robin.

Twenty-Ninth Entry

A bunch of us were in the suite and a few people were hollering for the Ouija board.

"Alf, go get the Ouija board, man, let's have a séance," this guy Tim barked at him. Because everyone treats Alf like a butler.

And if I wasn't drunk I probably would have been quieter when I said, "Alf you want me to get it?"

"No! Ha! I can get it!"

But I could see he was scared to go alone. Probably he was trying to impress milk-carton-pretty Robin, who he'd been talking to in the corner when that Tim guy demanded the board.

Alf left the suite and headed downstairs. I watched him over the bannister to make sure that nothing happened.

I knew the rub. Alf didn't.

I'd seen the others. He had no idea.

I'd seen Sybil and Margaret and could handle anything else the house had in store, but Alf, he couldn't. He'd gotten so scared he'd peed himself. I should tell Robin that.

He retrieved the Ouija board from the closet without a hitch, then came back upstairs and put it down between a bunch of us.

And I thought about when it had just been me and him up here, sitting over this same Ouija board, and we both had our coffees and he was smiling and we were having fun. It suddenly seemed so quiet in here. Thinking about it. Like someone had poured last night right into my ears.

Last night Alf had asked me what was wrong. What's wrong? What's wrong, Noelle? No one had ever really asked me that and wanted to help so much before. What's wrong? And he even took me all the way into the basement. Where I left him because I'm bad. I'm bad. I'm not good to my father, I hate him, a sick old man and I want to leave him just like I left Alf in the middle of the night to do god knows what.

Maybe I did try to kill Herman.

But he's not a sick old man. He's not, Noelle. He's perfectly fucking fine, just a

selfish lazy prick. WHO LIED TO YOU.
WHO IS A LIAR.

Shut up, diary.

SHUT UP.

I don't need to hear it from you, okay? I
know he's sick in the head, alright? I get that.
But he's still a fucking liar.

Anyway, there were four of us at the
Ouija board. Me and Alf and that annoying
Robin girl. She's been hanging around him
all night. I heard them laughing and they sat
really close on the couch for a long time.

And Alf's other kind of friend, Rod.
A nice guy, kind of nerdy like Alf. He was
gonna play with the Ouija board too.

We all put our hands on the planchette
and I felt a quiver run through me. Not
fear but something else, the memory of
Sybil's cold body sitting next to me in this
very room. And I think Alf felt it too, only
he wouldn't realize that chill was Sybil. He
would just think he was scared. He looked
up at me with big eyes.

Rod and Robin were pestering him to
start asking questions.

And Alf was regretting this decision.
This decision to tell people about the Ouija
board. He was too scared to keep going and
he wanted me to help.

"Okay, Alf, if it's okay with you I'm going to take the reins here. Just going to ask it some general questions first. You know, get it warmed up," I said.

Alf exhaled and said, "Be my guest."

"Alright." I sat up straighter and continued. "Is Alf gay?"

And Rod and I pushed it over to YES before Alf had the chance to realize what we were doing and Alf realized that I was helping him by turning the whole Ouija board thing into a big joke before anyone got too serious about it. But also I was trying to make him look like a nerd in front of that Robin girl. Yeah I know, I know. I'm mean. Don't start.

"Alf, you're cheating!" I stood up and pointed at him.

"I am not!"

"You are! You were pulling it towards NO. Alf, this doesn't work unless you're serious about it."

"Oh come on, you idiots!"

"Okay, okay, let me ask it a question," and Rod took over. "Will Alfred go and get us all beers." And we all held the pointer on YES while Alf again tried to pull it toward NO. Again defeated.

"Cripes, Alf!" I exclaimed. "I thought you

had respect for the dead. Cheating at a game like this, my god."

"Okay, but Noelle, you've gotta come down and help me because you're an asshole."

"Okay fine."

We got up to leave the room, both of us kind of drunk and unsteady. Alf put his arm over my shoulder.

I knew they might toy with the Ouija board for a while but eventually lose interest because nothing in this house would PERFORM, would give them the SUPERNATURAL EXPERIENCE that they wanted. The house would prefer them to look like fools when they lied and said they'd felt something graze their arm in the bathroom alone, or that they'd seen something move down in the dark lobby.

And then it just happened. Before I knew it I'd pulled Alf into one of the rooms. And his lips were on mine and they were so soft and sweet and it was a kiss. And it felt really good. He tasted sort of like beer, but also sort of like laughing. I know how dumb that sounds but I really felt like I could taste how funny he was all over his mouth. And so we kept kissing and kissing and Alf had my cheeks in his hands and he pulled my face back, looking me in the eyes.

I didn't want Alf to be around that Robin girl anymore. Alf was mine. He would be my friend forever, no matter what. No matter if tonight, just once, we fooled around.

"Noelle, you're great."

"No I'm not, Alf." For god's sake, I think I'm only doing this so that you don't have sex with Robin. And to reward you, I suppose, for manning up and coming to the party because we want you here.

We want you here.

We, like me and the diary and Sybil. We're all happy that you wanna stay here, work at the inn forever. It's what you want and we can make your wish come true.

"You are," he continued, though I tried to shut him up with long, laughing kisses. "I think you're just the best, Noelle. I really do."

"Well, thanks Alf. But then why are you talking to Robin?"

"To be nice! She doesn't know anyone here really. Ha! Were you jealous?"

"No!"

"Noelle, I love you," and then I could feel his hands shaking on either side of my face and it made me laugh. Then he laughed.

"Alf, you're my best friend."

"You're my best friend."

And then we started kissing again. And I pulled Alf towards the bed because I didn't want to keep talking about how he loved me, I didn't want to have to say anything back. I just wanted to have sex with him. But a small part of me wanted to burst into tears. Because after this we might not be friends anymore. And the kissing was really nice, better than I'd expected. And I suddenly realized that I trusted Alf. I trusted him the way I trusted my dad with a Q-tip in my ear. I trusted him that he'd wanna be friends with me no matter what. Because I had to, because here we are. About to have sex probably. About to have sex definitely.

The party thundered outside. Because it was a great fucking party, with its own momentum.

Alf was suddenly naked, and so was I, and he was kissing me and saying things like, "Are you sure you wanna do this? Oh Noelle, I've wanted this to happen for so long."

And I didn't really know what to think about that.

My sore spot throbbed, excited for the balm because it always felt good and calm when I was having sex with someone. I pressed into my bloody scalp with the heel of my palm and then Alf and I hugged so hard we both burst into patterned space and bobbed along for a while like there was no one else here.

After it was done I said he was just a pervert now, instead of being a virgin pervert. And he laughed. He laughed. So I guess I'm allowed to make fun of him again for being a pervert. Which is nice. It really is.

Now I'm sitting in the closet and writing because that just fucking happened. Alf and I had sex. We had fucking SEX. ME AND ALF. And I don't know who else to tell about it. And I don't know what to do now.

— I want it so super red in there that she barely looks human.

Everything seems totally fine. It really does. Probably Alf's so excited he could die. And I'm glad I could make him so happy. I am.

I've got a beer in here and it's sort of fun to drink it alone. I've never had a drink alone before.

Aaaaaaaaaaaaaaaand drunk.

Andrea was in Alf's room with that Bill guy. I gave her a key which maybe I shouldn't have. I told Alf and he laughed instead of getting mad so I guess it's okay.

There are people just outside in the hallway drinking and I don't want them to know I'm in here. I don't want them asking any questions. So I'm going to wait till they leave. These two girls from my school. Sisters. Ariel and Brittany, and though they aren't conjoined they may as well be. No one will ever be attracted to either of them and a childhood accident left them each uniquely disfigured. Ariel has a fake eye and Brittany can't grow hair. They're good-natured though. And not in the annoying way that disfigured people can often be, the way they are on the shows that Herman watches on TV.

When I left the suite, June was lying on the floor in front of the speaker and flipping through CDs and kind of letting people come up and talk to her. She had this idea that she could get more drunk lying down. She said she'd tested the theory so who was I to tell her it was stupid.

Thirtieth Entry

My closet doesn't feel so small after the party.

A few people are sleeping over, which is not going to go over well with Jessica tomorrow but I don't really care right now. She'll come in early, she might have a little fit but then I'll cry and I'll show her the scab on my head and I'll beg her not to tell Olivia and hopefully she'll feel bad enough for me that she won't.

Last I checked, Dwayne was passed out on the lawn, but he might have wandered home by now.

Brittany and Ariel are sleeping in the lobby on that dirty swirling carpet. Fucking gross. I literally have no idea when someone last vacuumed it. It might, honestly, have been years. Alf and I say we did it, and check off this little box behind the front desk saying we did all this cleaning stuff, but honestly I don't even know where the vacuum is.

Andrea and Bill were going to sleep in Alf's room. Sorry, Alf, that's completely my fault. And they're definitely going to have sex in your bed.

Alf and I are going to sleep in my bed. Together. He's up there now, probably sound asleep already. And it's going to feel nice not to be alone. And I hope it's fine tomorrow. I really do. He did what I wanted him to. He came to the party and it was great. Robin left. And nothing bad happened. I knew that the house would behave.

I didn't just sleep with him because he came to the party, diary. Okay? I'm not a fucking COMPLETE monster beast. Okay? Alf and I are best friends. I would never do that. And it wasn't just because of that Robin girl either, or his new jeans.

Maybe I love Alf. Maybe I do. Maybe maybe maybe I do.

Goddamnit, diary, would you stop judging me for god's sake? Ever since I picked you up you've been a total bitch. Making me write down all the things that are weird and bad about me, leaving it out like a big fat bloody vein waiting for someone to rip it open, read it and kill me.

You haven't been my better self at all. You've been just terrorizing my regular self. Ever since I started using you, I've been fucking crazy.

You're the reason, diary, you're the reason all of this is happening. You're working with the house. You are. The house knew that bathroom light, that door closing in my room was just enough to get me writing. It knew about you all along.

And you made me look at myself in this terrible horrible way, see and know that I should have never been fucking born, making me scratch away at that fucking thing in my brain, my skull showing now I'm sure of it and I wanna break it. I really do. I wanna break it like a windowpane.

The house wants it. You made it happen. You're bad. You don't love me. You're just as bad as me, turning on your mother and your father.

Okay I'll write it down because why not. Because why not just do it. These diaries, these girly little things, always judging always judging, little girls taught to judge everything, lie about themselves already, writing in the diary, omitted, things omitted but right there always, ever-present OTHER, you're an OTHER, a JUDGING OTHER built into me, right into my brain because you are me, my TRUEST ME DIARY DIARY DIARY DIARY confess, confess, CONFESS! Writing writing writing torture. Fuck you, diary. FUCK YOU FUCK YOU FUCK YOU FUCK YOU FUCK YOU FUCK YOU FUCK YOU!

A loud crash sound down in the basement.

But I know that no one else really heard it because everyone's drunk and passed out or having sex upstairs, not listening, not paying attention to the house like me, in one of its most secret insides. Most secret insides. Our closet under the stairs. Inside the house and a part of the house like we've got the same parts, the same stuff flowing through us and out of the hole in my head.

Small metallic clank.

One. Okay just one. Maybe it's nothing.

Another one. Okay two. Just two.

Three. Shit.

Four.

Clanks coming up the basement stairs. Louder. Louder. Louder as it gets closer to the main floor.

Five. Six. Seven. Eight. Faster.

It would be at the basement door now.

Fuck, fuck, fuck. And I heard the sound of the latch, too slow.

And then hissing. Like a board game hourglass, something heavy being dragged along the filthy carpet. Down the hallway, just outside the closet door, but moving past it now. What the fuck.

Margaret. Margaret. Margaret is looking for me. She's going to fucking kill me. Sammy must be dead. He must not have survived after he fell from my arms to the hard basement floor.

Am I asleep now? Did I fall asleep in the closet? No I'm awake. I'm definitely fucking awake. This isn't patterned space, this is real space. So maybe she can't hurt me. Maybe I'm just drunk and imagining things. I won't sleep tonight. I'll stay awake all night so nothing bad will happen to anyone. Because they can't leave patterned space. But they can. Because we talked to Sybil or someone on the Ouija board. Someone moved that real life planchette. They can do whatever they want, wherever they want, whenever they want.

I'm never ever coming back here again. Just like you warned me, Sybil. You warned me I should never ever come back. I'm leaving now and never coming back. Just gotta wait. Gotta wait for her to go away, then I'll run. First I'll get Alf though, I'll get Alf and then we'll run out the door. And if we can't run out the door, we'll jump out a window if we have to, make one of those weird ropes out of ripped sheets that people make in movies.

And then so loud, up the stairs over top of me. The rumbling thunder of that metallic something dragged up, thud, thud, thud against the carpeted steps. And then CRACK! CRACK! CRACK! Snapped wood, something tearing. More dragging. CRACK! CRACK! CRACK! CRACK! CRACK! CRACK! So many this time. Is she crashing through the rooms looking for me? Is she going to hurt Alf? I put my hand on the knob and want to go save him but I'm terrified, my whole body paralyzed.

She can't hurt anyone. If she could, she would have. Last night when Alf was alone with her in that room in the basement, she could have killed him then if she'd wanted to.

It was me she wanted. She was looking for me, coming to kill me, this is how I'll be punished. And then I'll be stuck in this house forever, she'll punish me for all of eternity.

Goddamn you Herman, why did you give me this life. Why did you make me live? You see it now. You see why I should have never been born. I made you see it. I'm going to make you see it.

She's back down the stairs.

Loud and faster than before. Is that fucking breathing? I picture her face, the black-and-white face I saw in the newspaper at the library, it's winded and wheezing, spittle hanging from its black-and-white dotted lip.

Her face that night at the inn, glistening with sweat, eyes made small, distorted by puffy flesh.

More thuds. Massive ones. Splintered wood.

JESUS. JESUS. FUCK FUCK FUCK.

The light just turned off. The light is off in here. FUCK. FUCK. The lights are off now and I can't see to write. I can't see.

FUUUUUUUUUUUUUCK!

I'm going to die. She's gonna fucking kill me. She wants to KILL ME. Sybil, someone HELP ME HELP ME DIARY!!!!!!!!!! 58

---

58 It should be noted that in this last section, Noelle's handwriting gets bigger and more frantic, begins to transform into what it looks like during her fugue states. At the bottom of the last page is a dark concentration of scribble in black pen, ripping a hole right through it and through the next few pages as well.

Hello again Mr. Dalrymple,

If you're reading this part that means you've made it to the end, and you're probably curious as to what happened next.

It was a crime scene with curiously little physical evidence, especially considering the amount of blood. Blood usually has a way of acquiring footprints and fallen hairs, but this blood didn't have any of that. Not a single print of any kind. The murderer would have had to put in considerable effort to achieve this. Particularly given the smeared blood trails from room to room, created by the bloody pickaxe dragging along the floor.

There were incredibly high blood alcohol levels in each of the bodies, which would explain the lack of defensive wounds—likely the victims weren't able to react quickly, if they woke up in time to react at all.

Noelle's body, found in the closet, presents an even more confusing array of evidence. For one thing, she had traces of all of the other victims' blood on her body, and not simply because she was murdered with the same weapon either. The traces of blood found on her suggest strongly that she was present during each of the murders, or at the very least interacting with the bodies postmortem. In addition, hers are the only prints found on the pickaxe. However, we can't understand how it would have been physically possible for her to have lodged that pickaxe into her head all by herself, and so accurately too. It was lodged directly into the "sore spot" she refers to so often in the diary.

We spent a lot of time investigating circumstances under which seemingly impossible feats of physicality can occur, particularly the occurrence of feats of physicality during sleepwalking and fugue states. Opinions on this matter are starkly divided.

Regardless, that Noelle murdered the rest of the kids was ultimately the most plausible theory based on the physical evidence at the inn.

And what we found in the Dixon home was more compelling still.

After many attempts to contact Herman Dixon via phone, an officer went to the house to find the front door open. He went inside and discovered Herman Dixon asphyxiated in his bed.

He too had been murdered within the last 48 hours. Strangled.

The size of the bruises on his neck were small, indicating that the murderer was likely a young female.

Again, there were no defensive wounds, but in this case they were puzzling. If Noelle had indeed strangled her father, the evidence at the house suggested that he might have let her.

Transcripts of the diary, with my annotations, were distributed to three child psychologists, one paranormal psychologist, and a handwriting expert (who reviewed a photocopy of the original diary as well). Many theories were presented, but none without flaws. Ultimately we closed the case naming Noelle as the murderer, but like I said, to this day I'm not convinced.

Without a living person to punish, the victims' parents filed a suit against the owners of the inn and lost. As far as I know, the place is still open and operating as it did back in 1999. In fact, this case probably renewed interest from the "novelty visitors" Noelle mentioned in the diary.

And we were never able to locate the Rat Pack. Not even Sammy. ——————————————

Fucking great Trevor. Fucking great. Okay, so I think I see what's happening here. In our version ,though, Noelle is going to be just another victim. Another poor sap who is trying to figure out the history of the house, but by the time she does it's TOO LATE. Margaret has already summoned her son to kill everyone.

So, first things first. Find Wink and Margaret's kid, get him to sign off. The first amendent can only take us so far, we've gotta be careful about defamation, right to privacy, blah blah blah. Obviously we won't use real names, but we want to cover our asses. I'm enclosing a release with these notes. Get him to sign it so we can make him everyone's worst nightmare next summer. Call me when you've found him.

And be careful, in case he really is a nutbar.

Acknowledgments

Thanks to Ali McDonald, Sam Hiyate, and Brian Farrey-Latz for continuing to believe in me.

Thanks to Tom, Debbie, Alex, Maddy, Sammy, and Teejee for absolutely everything—don't think I could have kept myself on track last year without you guys.

A super extra special thanks to my favorite deputy, for seeing lots of scary things and living to tell the tale.

And finally a belated thanks to the great Kennedy Cullen, whose editorial eye is good enough to eat.

Photo by Paul Clairmont

About the Author

Ainslie Hogarth was born and raised in Windsor, Ontario, but currently resides in Toronto. She has an undergraduate degree in English Literature and Philosophy and a Masters in Creative Writing. She watches a lot of movies and has a lot more books in her head. Visit her online at ainsliehogarth.com.

Don't miss Ainslie Hogarth's
Flux debut, *The Lonely*.